Murd

Gary Comenas

Copyright 2021 Gary Comenas
Published 2021 Jackleton Press

Table of Contents

1. Crumville — 5
2. New York — 10
3. Sluggo's — 17
4. Blunt — 20
5. Gigi's — 25
6. The Photographer — 29
7. The Photoshoot — 36
8. The Hit — 45
9. Mr. Wang's — 49
10. José — 59
11. The Hole in The Wall — 64
12. Disco! — 68
13. Lieutenant Warren — 72
14. Ava and Luigi — 77
15. The Downfall — 85
16. The Plan — 94
17. The Attic — 103
18. Mission Accomplished — 109
19. The Blonde Next Door — 114
20. The Date — 122
21. The Getaway — 129
22. The Cop-Killer — 133
23. Candy on the Beach — 138
24. Ginger's — 144
25. A New Identity — 150
26. Warren Gets Lucky — 157
27. Candy, Sweet Candy — 160
28. A Shadow — 164
29. Las Palmas — 171
30. Las Vegas — 174

1. Crumville

Writing isn't easy with a bullet stuck in the back of your head, but I'm determined to get my story down before it's too late. Not that anyone cares. Most of my family are gone now, but maybe, someday, someone in the future will want to know what really happened to me, to my father, to everyone involved. I don't think I'm a bad person. I might have killed some people, but I don't feel like a bad person inside. I should have never moved to New York. That's where it all started going wrong, and right...

* * * * *

As Conchita Alvarez made her daily rounds in the Hospital Las Palmas, she noticed that one of her patients had dropped a black notebook on the floor. After quickly rifling through it and seeing that it was written in English, she left it in a drawer in his bedside table.

'He should be writing in Spanish,' she said to herself. 'People who live in a foreign country should learn how to speak the language. Pretty soon there won't even be a Spanish language. Everyone in the world will be speaking American.'

She looked at his medical notes: "Blake Webster, 23 years old." Still young. She checked to see the time of his last injection – about four hours ago – and wondered why the hospital wasn't just feeding the morphine through the tube in his neck with his other meds. "Hey Blake!" she said as she got ready to inject him. His eyes opened slightly. Pointing to the syringe she was holding, she loudly announced "Morphina!"

He smiled and said in bad Spanish, "tee queero," meaning *te quiero* – 'I love you.' She laughed. At least he was trying to speak the language. Maybe he wasn't such a bad guy after all. She practiced her English: "Gib me your leg" she said, meaning 'give me your arm.'

Blake watched as she slowly inserted the needle into his vein until the blood swirled upwards into the barrel, indicating that she had found a vein. As she pushed the plunger down, Blake felt the warmth of the morphine working its way through his body until he no longer felt any pain. "Más, mas!" he joked.

She was surprised by his reaction and wondered whether he was a criminal or a victim. It's not every day that you get a 23-

year-old patient with a bullet lodged in the back of their head. She remembered that when he arrived that afternoon, there was another man in the ambulance with him who she thought was a cop. He was wearing a raincoat, even though it wasn't raining, and his shoes were black and shiny, like a policeman's shoes. He talked to the doctors with an American accent, and they gave Blake a private room. Maybe he was rich. They hadn't restrained him in any way, so it was doubtful he was a criminal.

She had been told that the doctors had left the bullet embedded in the back of his skull because removing it would make things worse. She watched him fall asleep under the influence of the morphine, with a smile on his face. 'No, not a bad person,' she thought, even though he was a foreigner. 'Not a bad looker either, even with a bullet in his head.' She giggled. He looked familiar, like she had seen him in a magazine. Maybe he was famous. She made a mental note to get a newspaper after work.

* * * * *

It may very well have been the case that the nurse had, at one time or another, seen a picture of Blake Webster in a magazine. He had been a professional model in New York before arriving in the Canary Islands, and he was also the face of Style Raven; a range of men's grooming products that were sold in drug stores, supermarkets, and barber shops throughout the world. They were meant to appeal to Mr. Average except Mr. Average didn't have Blake's striking blue eyes, wavy black hair or sculpted cheekbones. But if Style Raven's customer base didn't look like Blake, they could at least share in the glamorous lifestyle he represented by using their products. Their trademark image was a close-up of his cleanly shaven face against a New York skyline.

Blake had begun his modelling career after moving to New York from a small desert town in California called Ridgecrest. A lot of the older people in the town, and there were plenty of them, still referred to it by its original name, Crumville – "Crum" being the surname of the founding family of the town. It seemed an appropriate name for a community populated by the ageing crumbs of humanity who called it home. Some of those ageing crumbs had, through no effort of their own, become millionaires after oil was discovered on some of the properties.

Blake's father was one of them. His farm didn't produce a huge amount of oil, but it was enough to make him a millionaire. It sure beat growing avocados which had been his previous source of income.

Blake's father had nothing to do with the company that was drilling the oil; he just sat back and reaped the rewards. Nobody in town noticed any difference in him after he became a millionaire. He didn't suddenly start driving around in a Rolls Royce or dressing up in fancy clothes. In fact, he went out of his way not to draw attention to himself. He lived in the same house he lived in before and drove the same pick-up truck he always drove. The only time that eyebrows were raised was when he went on a trip to Palmdale and came back with an 18-year-old adoptee named Brooke who he quickly, and discretely, married in a civil ceremony with only two witnesses invited – his lawyer and his bank manager. Brooke later gave birth to Blake.

Young brides weren't that unusual in Ridgecrest after oil was discovered. Other residents got used to seeing the young family during the rare times they went into town. At least Brooke and the son were young; John Webster was nearing sixty when he got married. Brooke's adoptive parents certainly didn't care about the age of her husband. They were just glad to be rid of her. She had spent most of her teenage years ditching school and driving around with older boys, smoking dope. The police had brought her home several times, high on God knows what, laughing uncontrollably.

Brooke thought her biological mother would be proud of her for snaring a millionaire, except that she didn't know who her biological mother was. Most of Brooke's background disappeared when she was handed over to an orphanage by the hospital that she was born in. She stayed in the hospital long enough to overcome a physical addiction to heroin that she had inherited from her mother who left the hospital soon after her daughter was born, anxious to get back to her work as a prostitute.

Brooke's greatest pleasure in life was spending money; John's greatest pleasure was counting it. He never asked himself what he was saving for, he was just addicted to saving and counting. Day after day after day.

Most of the oil money went into his regular bank account and was legitimately accounted for, but over the years he had also managed to skim off more than a million dollars in tax-free cash which he kept in a safe in the attic, along with expensive jewellery from second-hand dealers who were happy not to have to explain where it came from. What the jewellery looked like was largely irrelevant. He purchased it by weight and carat. Like the skimmed cash, it was a form of exchange that he never exchanged.

He rarely allowed his wife to wear the jewellery, but it was so ugly and tasteless, she didn't mind. Sometimes he let her watch him count the contents of the safe and it was during one of those evenings that she left him. When John took a break in his counting to go to the bathroom, she scooped up as much of his bounty as she could and split. She just couldn't take it anymore. As far as she was concerned, she had married the most boring person in the world.

Blake was six years old when his mother left. His father ignored her disappearance as much as he had ignored her presence. There were no photographs of her in the house or any other trace of her existence. John Webster never reported her for the theft, for fear that it might bring attention to the remaining contents of the safe. He had no problem replacing the tax-free cash and jewellery she took with more tax-free cash and jewellery.

When Blake was ten, a couple of policemen visited his father. He overheard them talking about his mother who had been busted for prostitution and was sitting in a jail cell in Manhattan. The cops asked if Blake's father wanted to post bail for her. He told them to leave her in jail. Nobody in Ridgecrest gave a damn about Brooke Webster. They were glad to see her go. Buxom blondes didn't fit in with the rest of the population.

Sometimes Blake tried to recall what his mother looked like, but all he could remember was the smell of her dark red lipstick when she kissed him goodnight or how she would dye her hair in the kitchen sink. She loved watching old movies on television and would often sing show-tunes while she did the housework in a fancy dress that would normally be reserved for evening wear. She didn't need evening wear. She and her husband never went out at night.

Blake's childhood memories consisted mostly of the sound of drilling by the oil pumps outside, and the constant beatings from his father who blamed him for his mother's disappearance. "Maybe if you hadn't been born, she would have stayed around longer" was the gist of the argument. According to his father "she wasn't the motherly type." Blake couldn't understand why he got all the blame. He didn't ask to be born, did he?

One childhood memory stuck in Blake's head more than any other. He was about eleven years old and had interrupted his father in the attic. The safe was open and the jewellery in it glistened like a pirate's treasure chest. But his father wasn't looking at the jewellery. He was sitting on a stool in the middle of the room, looking at pictures in porn magazines that were spread around him on the floor. His hand was covered by a pair of black lace panties, presumably belonging to his departed wife, and he was masturbating over the pictures. Blake ran out of the room when his father saw him, but it was too late. His father dragged him back into the room and sat him on his lap, telling him not to worry. It was the most comforting he had ever been.

John Webster turned his son's head downward and forced him to look at the sea of porn surrounding them. He talked about the pictures as if he was educating his son about sex. Then Blake felt a wetness underneath him, as if his father had spilt something, and heard him moan slightly. When his father finished moaning, he started slapping Blake, telling him he was a bad boy before pushing him off his lap onto the floor. When he stood up, his father hit him again and Blake ran to the door. As he went down the stairs, he could hear his father shouting "Mommy's boy" after him.

His father never repeated the sexual abuse, but he did repeat the beatings. God forbid if Blake ever asked about his mother. Then his dad would really get angry. He would take off his belt and swat his son mercilessly with it, sweat pouring down his face, blaming him for every misfortune in his own life.

As soon as Blake turned twenty-one, he left home without saying where he was going, just as his mother had done. But unlike his mother, he left a note behind. It consisted of three sentences: "I hate you. You're disgusting. Good-bye."

The next time that Blake's father saw his son's face, it was on the side of a can of shaving cream.

2. New York

There was only one city where Blake wanted to go. New York. He had read so much about it on the internet, and it seemed like a magical place where anything could happen. 'Who knows?' he thought. He might even find his mother there. He never forgot the visit by the cops who told his father that she was in Manhattan. It was a long time ago, but maybe she would still be living there. Manhattan didn't seem that big when he looked it up on a map on the net. The people who lived there weren't supposed to be very friendly, but what town could be less friendly than Crumville? He had got used to being the brunt of jokes as he grew up because he was so tall and skinny. "Hey, where's your beanstalk Jack?" older kids would shout out from their cars. What could be worse than that?

Blake took a Greyhound bus to New York. It was scary being on his own. He knew he'd never go back to Ridgecrest, he'd never travelled such a distance before. The initial excitement he felt when he left home – the feeling of freedom – was quickly replaced by boredom. He had brought a notebook with him to document his trip but there was nothing to document. Whenever he looked out the window all he could see were dull expanses of wheat-fields, particularly when they hit the mid-west. Texas seemed to go on forever. He hoped he would meet some interesting people on the bus, but they all looked so tired, like they had been travelling for most of their lives and just wanted to left alone. A few of them were drinking out of bottles when the driver wasn't looking, but he probably wouldn't have cared. He looked just as worn out as they did.

He experienced a completely different feeling when the bus finally arrived at the Port Authority building in Manhattan. When he got out of the Port Authority building, he just stood on the steps mesmerised by, well, everything. The tall, grey buildings looked just like they did on old crime films he watched on TV as a kid. He'd never seen so many people coming and going. It was like he had left the dullest town in the world to arrive in the most exciting one - like his life had suddenly gone from slow motion to fast. He hadn't booked a room in advance, but he wasn't worried about it. He knew he would find somewhere to live. For the first time in his life, he really felt like he belonged somewhere. He even knelt down and kissed the sidewalk. People smiled at him as they passed like they knew how he felt, like they knew New York was the greatest place in the world.

He found a cheap hotel near Times Square, not far from the Port Authority. It was called The Broadway. It looked like it was about to collapse but that didn't worry him. He knew they wouldn't let people stay there if that was the case. He was mostly attracted by the handwritten sign in the window that said, "weekly rates available." He figured it would be cheaper to pay by the week. He had to be careful with his money. He had about two thousand dollars in cash on him which he had saved up by stocking shelves at Walt's Mart back home and it had to last until he got a job.

He looked through the hotel window from the sidewalk and saw the back of a large black woman standing behind a desk. Several hanging bells rattled as he walked through the door. Somebody was already talking to her at the desk, presumably a customer, so he patiently waited his turn.

"Listen Jonesy," the big woman behind the desk was saying in a deep voice. "I don't care why you don't have the money; the management needs your rent. They're hassling me and they don't do it nicely. You can't even be bothered to think up a new excuse. How many times can one person get mugged in this city?"

"New York is a dangerous place, Miss Carlotta."

Carlotta had had enough. She banged her bracelet-laden arm down on the desk and stared at him in his one eye that worked.

"That's it. I have had enough. Pack your bags and go. I'm fed up with your lies."

"But Miss Carlotta, you know I'm good for the money. I just need a bit more *time*."

"Time! HOW MUCH TIME? You lookin' like you'll barely make it 'til tomorrow. Ain't you goin' to the clinic anymore?"

"Well, the story about the clinic is..."

"No! I can't take it anymore! You have one week left. I don't care how you get the money - all the money - but get it. Rob a bank for God's sake or steal an old lady's purse. Otherwise, you're out. Do you understand? O.U.T, out! My career is at stake!"

By "career" she meant her career as a hotel desk clerk.

Carlotta pushed Jonesy aside and screamed "Next!" looking at Blake. Her anger softened considerably when she saw what he she was looking at. Not many young, good-looking men wanted to stay in that dump. 'He looks like a model - probably a hustler,' she thought.

"Good morning," she said with an exaggerated smile as she leaned forward, pressing her breasts against the counter to full effect. Those breasts cost a fortune and she was determined to make the best of them.

Morning? Blake looked at the clock above the desk. It was 4 pm.

"Good morning," he responded, politely.

"I do apologise that you had to witness that awful tirade. I'm not usually like that," she said in the gentle voice she had been taught to use after the operation that had turned her from a man to a woman.

"Are you a model?" she asked, flutteringly her false eyelashes.

"No ma'am. I'm looking for a room."

'Hmmm. A hustler then,' she decided. Judging from his drawl he was probably some hick from the mid-west looking for fame and fortune while making a few bucks on the side until he was 'discovered.' She'd been in a similar situation when she first arrived from New Orleans over thirty years ago.

"Okay, honey. Just so you know, what you do in your room is your business, but we don't tolerate violence of any type in this hotel, and we do co-operate with the police when absolutely necessary. Otherwise, I hear no evil, see no evil and certainly don't speak no evil. Got it?" she said with a wink.

Blake liked Carlotta. You didn't get characters like her in Crumville.

"Are you on methadone, baby?" she asked out of the blue.

"Methadone!" He didn't know a lot about methadone, but he thought it was a type of heroin.

"No, of course, I'm not on methadone. Why would you think that?"

"I thought you might be a patient at that clinic on the corner. Some of our most respectable residents are, you know. Those clinic patients - they always on time with their rent. Where you from, honey?"

"Ridgecrest. It's a small town in California."

"Can't say I've ever heard of it."

"It used to be called Crumville."

"I ain't definitely never heard of Crumville," she laughed. "I hail from New Orleans originally, but I've been managing this place for the past three decades, I'm afraid."

"You must have seen so many changes."

"Changes!" She seemed surprised at the suggestion. Grabbing a key card from under the desk, she told Blake to follow her down a musty hallway.

"Nah, I ain't seen many changes. Not really. I guess a lot of the welfare hotels became boutique hotels, but not this one." She laughed thinking about all the dives that were now "boutique" hotels. "As for the clientele, well they ain't changed at all. Different faces. Same old crimes. Same old hopes and dreams. You can become anything you want in New York, except a success."

When they reached Blake's room - number 9 - Carlotta tried to open the door with the key card without much success. Finally, she rubbed the bent card against the wall to flatten out the creases which seemed to do the job. "These things never work," she complained. "Dunno why they got rid of them metal keys."

She showed him the room. There wasn't much to show. A single bed with a sagging mattress was positioned against a wall with red stains that looked like they'd been squirted there by a junkie with a bad aim. Next to the bed was a small set of drawers with one leg missing that was propped up with a small stack of magazines. The top of the drawers served as a bedside table. Above that were electric outlets, including a USB port where a resident could charge their phone, providing it was old enough.

"No expense spared in this joint," Carlotta said. "We even got free wifi. And it's good wifi too. Nothing but the best for our residents."

Free wifi was important. Blake planned to do a lot of job hunting on his laptop.

Carlotta continued: "At $300 a week, the room is a bargain, especially in this rip-off city. In parts of New Orleans, you can still get a luxury apartment for that price."

They walked back to the front desk where Blake handed over $600 in cash for two weeks rent.

"Welcome to your new home," Carlotta said, as she handed over the key card. Holding her hand sideways at the edge of her mouth, like a stage whisper, she added, "If you is ever thirsty, Sluggo's next door is open to residents 24 hours. I'll give him your name."

"Thanks." Blake smiled as he walked to his room. 'Who on earth would need access to a bar 24 hours a day?' he wondered.

He had problems with the key card too - until he flattened it against the wall like he had seen Carlotta do. He used to have to do that to make dollar bills go through the vending machines they had in the cafeteria at Walt's Mart.

Inside his room he quickly unpacked and plugged in his laptop. He needed to find a job soon - before he ran out of money. He certainly wouldn't be able to depend on his father for financial support. John Webster had made it clear to his son while he was growing up that he would have to fend for himself in the world - that he should never expect any handouts. After all, John had never got any handouts, so why should his son? He forgot that it had been completely by luck that oil had been found on his property and wasn't the result of his own hard work. The company who discovered it paid him for the privilege of drilling it. All he had to do was collect the money.

John Webster reinforced his "fend for yourself" conviction by leaving his money to a donkey sanctuary in his will. He didn't give a damn about the donkeys, but it enabled him to remind Blake after his mother left, that he would rather give his millions to a bunch of asses than to his own son.

During the bus trip to New York, Blake could sometimes still hear the sound of his father's voice condemning him; it made him even more determined to make a success of himself. After connecting to the wifi in his room, he scoured the web for any unskilled jobs he could find. Most of the work was offered through agencies who requested that a resumé be attached to any email enquiries, but he didn't have a resumé. Instead, he included a short paragraph about what it was like to stack shelves at Walt's Mart. What he failed to realise, in all of his small-town innocence, was that he possessed the two qualities that New Yorkers craved the most: Youth and Beauty. Instead of including a paragraph about Walt's Mart, he should have attached a photo.

While he was online, he also checked out New York's nightlife. It was his first night in "the city that never sleeps" and he wanted to make the most of it. The only nightclub he had been to before was Jazzy's in Palmdale. It wasn't much fun but sometimes he would get lucky and find a girl who was willing to fool around in one of the booths. The music was mostly country and there was no dancing to speak of, but the skirts were short and after a few drinks that was the most important thing. Some of the girls – the ones who came with reputations that preceded them – didn't even wear underwear.

The New York club scene looked a lot more sophisticated than the scene in Palmdale. Blake made a list of all the clubs he wanted to check out and chose a place called Blunt as his first stop. Their website had a "What Happened Last Night" section with photographs from the previous night, showing how much fun everyone had on Wednesday night. There was no reason that Thursday night should be any less fun. And, best of all, they only charged $10 to get in. Every penny mattered until he got a job.

Having planned his evening, he left to get a takeaway pizza to bring back to his room. It would be cheaper than eating out. When he returned to the hotel, Carlotta, who seemed to live at the front desk, noticed the pizza box and stood up, holding her hand out, palm facing forward, like a traffic cop: "Uh-uh baby. No way. You ain't bringin' no pizza into this establishment. No siree. No eating in the rooms."

When Blake asked why, she told him it was because of the cockroaches: "They love pizza. They really do. Well, I guess they like anything edible, but especially pizza. It must be the cheese."

Cockroaches? She hadn't mentioned cockroaches when he handed over his two weeks rent. Nor had she mentioned the rule about not eating in his room. Instead of arguing like most New Yorkers would do, he apologised and took his pizza outside. He found a place to sit on the steps of a deserted office building and ate his pizza there, watching the world go by.

What a world it was. He'd never seen so many different types of people in one place, all rushing around as if their lives depended on getting to wherever they were headed; a never-ending stream of humanity hurrying to and fro, some dressed for the theatre, others for dinner and still others who were hardly dressed at all - girls hoping to lure a drunken tourist into an alleyway for some costly fun or to have one of their waiting friends rob him at knifepoint. He saw a man in a business suit yelling "Police! Police!" as he ran down the street, completely ignored by the other people hurrying past him. Everyone seemed to have such a purpose in life, like they were rushing to somewhere that they really needed to get to - except for Blake, of course, who ended up sharing his pizza with a tramp who had asked him for spare change.

When Blake got back to the hotel, Carlotta was still behind the reception counter, watching the twenty-four-hour news channel on television. "Sorry Blake, but there ain't no hotels in New York that would allow a pizza in a room, except the ones with room service of course. But we ain't got room service, at least not that sort of room service." There was that wink again. It was beginning to get on his nerves.

3. Sluggo's

Blake left his room at ten to go to Blunt. One person had commented on the club's website that it really didn't get going until midnight, so he thought he'd stop at Sluggo's for some liquid courage on the way. It was bound to be a lot cheaper than Blunt's. He didn't realise how cheap until he got into the place. Most of the clientele were considerably older than him and looked like they had spent most of their lives waiting for their next drink. Blake couldn't tell if the beads of sweat that glistened on their foreheads were the result of an out-of-control heating system or alcohol poisoning.

"What'll it be young man?" asked a bartender with bloodshot eyes and drooping skin, who turned out to be Sluggo, himself.

"I guess I'll have a screwdriver," Blake answered.

Sluggo poured him half a glass of vodka and added a small amount of orange juice "for color," as he put it. Blake gave him a two-dollar tip. Sluggo pulled a cord that rang a bell to signify that a tip had been given - something he had picked up when he was much younger and had travelled to England looking for an 'English rose,' but ended up with a thirty-day sentence for drunk and disorderly.

"Nice touch." Blake said, referring to the bell.

"I *knew* you were a foreigner," Sluggo observed. "Now let me see. Judging from the accent, I'd say you're from California way. Am I right?"

Blake laughed. "Got it in one."

"I knew you were from out of town even before you opened your mouth. Your clothes are definitely from out of town. Most of the 'flys' at this bar wear what they slept in last night. Your threads are almost devoid of wrinkles."

Blake was wearing his 'clubbing' clothes. The jeans he normally wore had been replaced by a pair of black wrinkle-resistant slacks, his sneakers with fake patent leather loafers.

Sluggo was always careful not to ask too many questions of newcomers. He realised that a simple question like 'how you doin?' could result in an hour's monologue about their past that tended to leave out all the juicy bits. Carlotta had already given him as much information about Blake as she knew - that he was probably just another small-town hustler who was trying his luck out in the big city.

Blake told Sluggo that he had just arrived in New York and was staying next door at the Broadway.

"I know," Sluggo answered. "Carlotta mentioned it. Good choice. Why spend money on a room when you can spend it on booze?"

Hustler or not, he hoped that Blake would become a regular. He was better looking than most of his clientele and would, hopefully, attract more women customers. That's what the bar needed - more women and more businessmen. At one point, Sluggo had put baskets of chicken wings on the bar hoping that it might attract a higher class of clientele, but all that happened was that drug addicts and drunks came in to eat the chicken and then went back on the streets to panhandle. When Blake finished his first drink, Sluggo gave him another one on the house.

"Gee, thanks." Blake said, giving him a thumbs up.

"Gee, you're welcome," Sluggo answered. "But before you get too excited, it doesn't mean you don't have to tip."

Blake laughed and handed over two dollars. "Sorry about that."

"So, where are we off to tonight?" Sluggo asked as he wiped down the dirty bar with an even dirtier cloth. "I'm sure you didn't get dressed up like that for this dive."

"I'm going to a club called Blunt. Do you know it?"

"Nah, I'm too old for clubs like that. I can still remember Studio 54. It wasn't too far from here."

"Oh, wow, I've read about Studio. Sounded like a wild place."

"Well, don't believe everything you read. It was kind of a PR scam. The celebrities walked in, got their pictures taken, and then walked out of a back door into their limos to go to a real party."

"Hey Johnny," he yelled to a person sitting away from the bar, on a chair in the corner of the room. His head was perilously close to his lap, and it was difficult to tell with his long blonde hair if he was male or female. Then you noticed the bald spot at the back of his head. "Remember Studio 54, Johnny?" Sluggo explained that Johnny used to be a regular there.

Johnny suddenly came to life and stared at them with pupils the size of pins. "Yeah, it was a fucking clip joint," he mumbled before nodding off again, a trail of saliva dripping from the side of his mouth. Sluggo touched Blake's arm to get his attention and imitated someone shooting up by way of explanation.

Blake was taken aback by Sluggo's imitation. He felt sorry for Johnny. He wondered how a human being could get himself into such a state but was too polite to say anything. He continued to make small talk - mostly about the difference between Ridgecrest and Manhattan - until he finished his second drink. When he got up to go, Sluggo suddenly got serious: "Blake, take some advice. You seem like a nice guy. New York has a way of destroying people. Don't let it happen to you. You don't want to end up like Johnny."

"Don't worry, I won't." Blake reassured him with his friendly, small-town smile. 'There's no way that I'd end up like Johnny,' he thought as he hit the streets of New York.

4. Blunt

Blunt was only a few blocks from Sluggo's. When he got there, Blake was surprised to see so many people trying to get in. He should have left earlier. A lot of people in the crowd were trying to get the attention of a woman in the front carrying a clipboard. "Eloise! Eloise!" they shouted, hoping she would let them in. Although the doormen and women at clubs like Blunt weren't as important as they had been during the days of clubs like Studio 54, they still wielded a considerable amount of importance. Everyone wanted to be on the "A" list.

Most of the door people were A-listers at other clubs, restaurants, and parties, but when they lost their job, they also lost their status and were largely ignored by their successors on the social scene. Usually, age had something to do with it - who wants a 60-year-old door person? The previous door person at Blunt had been put out to pasture as soon as she reached 60. She committed suicide after a few non-successful attempts at reinventing herself as a journalist and was later found hanging from her shower rail at home, next to her wedding dress.

Eloise had lasted longer than most, but she was in her mid-fifties now and her days were numbered. For the time being, however, the years she had spent as an A-lister gave her an insider's knowledge of who was "in" (and who wasn't) which was indispensable for someone like Blunt's owner, Howie Morgan. Eloise took care of the customers who had already attained their place on the A list while Howie tried to find the A-listers of the future. On most nights he joined Eloise in the front of the club for at least part of the evening, choosing new customers who weren't 'on the list' yet, but were either too gorgeous or outrageous to ignore. He had his own wooden box in front of the club - nicknamed his 'soapbox' - that he stood on to get a good view of everyone. He was standing on his soapbox when Blake arrived.

"Hey, you!" he shouted in Blake's direction.

Blake looked behind him and then pointed at himself: 'Me?' he mouthed.

Howie laughed and said, "Yeah, you." He motioned for him to come forward.

Blake wondered what sin he had committed. He had grown up feeling guilty about most of his actions - his father had made sure of that - and he thought the guy on the box was going to ask him to go home and change. Everyone around him looked so dressed up, like pictures in a magazine.

He walked up to Howie and started to apologise: "I, um, I'm sorry. Did I do something wrong?"

"No, darling, you did something right. You were born. Get inside."

Blake attempted to hand over his $10 entry charge to Howie, only to be met by a blank stare. It made him nervous, and he started talking too much, thanking Howie too enthusiastically and explaining how it was his first night in New York, that he had just moved here from a small town called Ridgecrest and so on and so on.

"Are you for real?" Howie asked.

Blake stood there stumped, not knowing what to say.

"Yes, you're for real," Howie answered for him.

He told Blake to put his money away and handed him some drink tickets. "Have a good time - and welcome to the greatest city in the world!"

'What a friendly person,' Blake thought as he entered the club.

Once he was through the doors, Blake walked down a series of wide translucent steps that were lit from below by multi-coloured lights and ended up standing at the edge of a large dance floor with a bar to his right. He felt like he was entering Oz. Blinded temporarily from bright strobe lights coming from the DJ booth at the opposite end of the dance floor, he clung onto the rail of the bar like he was preparing for lift-off. While waiting to be served, someone grab his arm. It was Howie.

"Blake, don't bother with this riff-raff," he said, looking at all the people trying to get a drink. "Go upstairs to Nelson's Room. It's the VIP room. I'll call Rita and let her know you're on your way."

"Who's Nelson?"

"He used to film the underground scene in the '80s. The room upstairs was his editing suite. He died of a heart attack or something. Probably too much... (Howie imitated someone snorting coke). Just go up those stairs. Rita will be waiting for you."

As Howie got on his phone, Blake made his way up another stairwell; a plain, dimly lit, series of wooden steps that he wouldn't have noticed if Howie hadn't pointed them out. Rita was waiting for him at the top. She unhooked a thick red barrier rope and let him into the V.I.P room. It was so much nicer than the main floor - no loud music, small tables with white tablecloths and waiters in evening suits with bow ties. A long bar extended the length of the room and large paintings decorated the walls. Blake wondered why anyone would want a painting of a soup can on their wall. Rita guided him to the bar, thinking 'My god, Howie was right. He really is gorgeous.'

Blake ordered his usual drink - a screwdriver. He noticed that the customer next to him had tickets like the ones Howie had given him and was using them to pay for their drinks. 'So that's what they're for,' he thought. 'They're like the coupons they give out for free samples at the Strawberry Festival in Crumville.' His screwdriver came at the same time as a drink for a woman with long brown hair on the other side of him, so he gave the bartender two tickets to pay for both of their drinks. She clinked glasses with him, saying "cool, thanks" and went back to her friends.

That was his third screwdriver that evening. It wasn't long before he ordered a fourth. Why not? They were free, as long as his tickets held out. Howie had given him quite a few. It was a way of keeping the best-looking guys in the club in order to attract paying customers - male and female. Mid-way into his drink, the room became as blurred as his thoughts and he found himself dancing with the woman he had treated to a drink earlier. Usually, his shyness prevented him from having too much fun, but on that night, he just let himself go. He even made a funny face when the club photographer took a picture of him and the brunette on the dance floor.

When he got back to the bar, a stranger walked up to him and introduced himself: "Hi, I'm Phil."

The new person even put his hand out for a handshake. As he shook Phil's hand, he noticed he was wearing a chunky gold signet ring with the letter "C" embossed on it.

"I'm Blake," he said, with a friendly smile.

"Hey, I saw all the drink tickets you had earlier. Do you wanna do a trade? A drink for a line of blow? How about it?"

Blake wasn't even sure what "blow" was. He told Phil not to worry about trading anything, that he was happy to get him a drink: "That guy at the front gave me loads of free tickets."

Phil was impressed. "That's Howie. He owns the place."

"What'll you have, partner?" Blake asked. He had no idea

why he was suddenly talking like a cowboy, but it seemed to fit the occasion.

"A whiskey and coke would be good," Phil answered.

After being served, Phil motioned to Blake to follow him and led him into the men's room. At least the sign outside the door said it was the men's room, but it was so crowded with both sexes that it was difficult to tell. Some of the men were even dressed like women. "Wow," was all that Blake could say. He'd never seen anything like it.

He followed Phil into a cubicle and watched him as he took what he called a "wrap" out of his pocket and made two lines on the top of the toilet basin. After snorting one of them with a dollar bill, he handed the bill over to Blake: "Go for it."

Blake went for it. He inhaled the other line like Phil had done. He didn't know what to expect. He'd never had cocaine before.

"How do you feel?" Phil asked.

"Numb," he said. "My throat feels numb."

Phil laughed. "That's a good sign. Is this the first time you've done coke?"

"Yeah, I guess so."

At first Blake didn't feel much, but as they walked back to the bar, he seemed more energetic and talkative.

"Are you from Slick?" Phil asked, when they were back at the bar.

"Slick? What's that? I'm from Ridgecrest. It's a small town that used to be called..."

Phil left before he finished his sentence. He thought Blake was one of the models from the Slick Modelling Agency who hung out at the club, but as soon as he found out he was just some schmuck from a small town he had never heard of, he lost interest.

Blake hardly noticed. He was flying high by then, and it seemed like when one conversation ended, another began. No sooner was Phil gone than somebody took his place. Blake bought the new person a drink too. New Yorkers were so friendly, not at all what he had expected. He could have stayed at the club until closing time but when he threw up in the restroom, he decided it was time to go home.

On his way back to the Broadway, he was surprised to pass a diner that was still open at that time of the night, or morning. Two small spotlights lit up a sign above the door, saying

"Gigi's." Blake leaned against a large glass window and peered inside. In his drunken state, the restaurant looked almost magical. The walls were decorated with black and white photos from the past - glossy photos not print-outs - of overweight mothers playing with their children and men fooling around in overcoats. He wished his family had been like that. Some of the men must have been celebrities because a few of the photographs were autographed. Blake wondered who Dean Martin was. Then he caught a glimpse of himself in the window's reflection, looking like a drunk leaning against a window, and continued walking home.

5. Gigi's

Blake woke up the next morning trying to remember the night before. His first night in New York had left him with a feeling he had never felt before. How do you define the best night of your life?

He was determined to find a job so he could stay in the city, but first he needed a strong coffee. He remembered the café he saw last night – Gigi's – so he went there with his laptop. He found a small empty booth in the back and was approached by an elderly waiter with white, slicked back hair.

"What'll it be?" the old guy asked, pad and pencil in hand.

Blake hadn't been given a menu and was too shy to ask for one. He tried something uncomplicated: "A strong coffee and, um, a ham and cheese sandwich,"

"Do you want your panini toasted?"

"Excuse me?"

"Your panini, your sandwich. Do you want it toasted? Are you from out of town or something?"

"Well, yes, I am from out of town. I'm from Ridgecrest. A toasted sandwich would be okay."

"Ridgecrest? Never heard of it."

"It used to be called Crumville."

"What is this, *Candid Camera*?" the old man asked, pretending to look for a camera.

"What's *Candid Camera*?" Blake asked.

"Forget it, buddy. You're too young. I'll get you a toasted panini. And let me guess. A diet coke?"

Blake's head was throbbing by this point, and he really wanted something alcoholic - a 'hair of the dog.' "Would it be possible to get a glass of wine?" he asked.

"Now we are talking," the old man answered. He shouted over to a young man behind the main counter: "Bring this gentleman a glass of the house red. *Presto*! It's an emergency."

As Blake gulped down his wine, he looked at the pictures on the walls. One of the people looked familiar - a young boy who got older as the photographs got newer. He looked like the man who had taken his order and was now busy taking a "panini" out of its plastic packaging and toasting it in a sandwich toaster. When he brought it to Blake's table, Blake asked if he was the boy in the pictures.

"Yes, that's me. I own the place. I'm Luigi. When I was a kid, I could only say Gigi, so everyone called me Gigi. My father opened the restaurant and he named it after me - with my nickname."

Luigi didn't mention that the restaurant had been a popular meeting place for the mob until the five crime families that ruled New York were busted in a major round-up during the 1980s. The newspapers had made a big deal of it at the time, calling it the end of the mafia, but organised crime still operated in the area, often with the help of people like Luigi who cooperated with the police when it was necessary and with the criminals when it was essential.

"Is that your father?" Blake pointed to a man holding Gigi's hand in one of the photographs.

"Yes, that was my father."

"What happened to him?"

"He got shot in the back by this guy," Luigi said, pointing at another man wearing an overcoat in a picture further down the wall.

Blake was horrified. "I'm so sorry."

Luigi shrugged. "It happens."

"What happened to the guy that killed him?

"He got killed by this guy." He pointed out a man in a different picture.

"And what happened to him?"

"He got married and moved to Queens."

The families in the photographs didn't seem so friendly anymore.

As Luigi walked back to the sandwich counter, Phil – the guy that Blake had done "blow" with at Blunt the night before – walked into the restaurant. Blake noticed that he greeted Luigi like they were old friends and watched the two of them go through a pair of double doors at the end of the counter. Beyond the doors was a supply room which Luigi used as an office of sorts. It was also where he stored the boxes of Panettone that the restaurant was famous for. It came straight from Italy. Although the bread-like cake was considered a Christmas treat in Italy, Luigi sold it throughout the year. Deliveries arrived weekly and hidden inside quite a few of the cakes was the cocaine that small-time dealers like Phil sold in New York clubs. Phil was the nephew of Luigi. His real name was Filippo Rossi.

They weren't in the storeroom very long but when they came

out, Phil was carrying a Macy's shopping bag that he didn't have when he went in. He nodded 'hello' to Blake as he walked out the door.

Luigi came up to Blake's table a few minutes later.

"You know Phil?" he asked.

"Yeah, I met him at Blunt last night. Nice guy."

"Are you a model?"

That question again.

"I wish. I'm actually looking for a job. Got any vacancies?"

Luigi smiled. What a nice boy, and probably a hard worker. Maybe too nice. "I wish I could offer you something, but most of the people who work here are family members," he said, emphasising the word "family."

"Like the people in the pictures?" Blake asked.

"You could say that."

"Who's Dean Martin?" he asked pointing to the autographed photograph.

"Who's Dean Martin!!?" Luigi left the table, shaking his head and mumbling something about "kids today" as he went back to work behind the main counter.

When Blake went up to the counter to pay on his way out, Luigi fobbed him off. "No, my friend, it's on the house." He had a hunch about this guy. With those good looks he was bound to be a success in New York. He could be useful. And he was looking for a job which meant he needed cash.

"Thanks. That's really nice of you." Blake said as he walked out the door. People were so much nicer in New York than they were in Crumville.

* * * * *

Back in his room, Blake continued his job search online. He even checked the Blunt site to see if they had any openings. He was surprised to see a photograph of himself dancing with a young brunette, sticking his tongue out at the camera, in the "What Happened Last Night" section. Apparently, the brunette - the girl he had bought a drink for last night - was an up-and-coming actress who had a supporting role in a revival of a Broadway musical about people who couldn't pay their rent.

'What a weird idea for a musical,' Blake thought, not that he had ever seen one. He felt slightly embarrassed about the photograph. He would never have acted like that at home, but at the same time, he felt honoured in a strange sort of way that he had even been mentioned on the site. He'd never been mentioned on a website before. He would have loved to have sent the link to the page to his friends in Crumville, but he had never made any friends in Crumville.

He turned off his computer and spent most of the afternoon lying on his bed, thinking of the brunette. He hadn't planned to return to the club so soon but when night fell, he couldn't help wondering what it would be like on a Friday. It was probably a big night. He couldn't resist another night at Blunt.

6. The Photographer

It was still early when Blake got to the club – about 10 pm. Howie wasn't there that night, but Eloise was, and she remembered him. She waived him through and gave him some drink tickets, just as Howie had. He stopped at the downstairs bar - he wanted a drink before he braved Nelson's Room. Quite a few girls came up to him, saying they had seen his photo on the website and others just whispered to each other, "that was the guy on the website."

He liked the attention, but it also made him nervous. Thank God Phil arrived. 'At least he can keep me company,' Blake thought. 'At least he can get me a drink,' Phil thought.

Phil had also seen Blake's picture on the website dancing with the almost famous actress. He wished that he could be in the "What Happened Last Night" section at least once. He'd been going to that club for a couple of years now and nobody ever took his picture. Given what he did for a living, he should probably have been grateful, but a little attention wouldn't hurt. He supposed he was sort-of famous as a dealer but only to his customers. If he ever stopped dealing, that would be the end of his fame.

"You're almost a star," he said to Blake as he ogled the giggling girls across from them. "Got any drink tickets?"

As soon as Blake got Phil a drink, one of Phil's friends came up to him and whispered something into his ear.

"I'll see you later - upstairs," Phil said, as he left to sort out his friend.

Blake was disappointed; he had been hoping for some company at the bar. He felt stupid standing there on his own, especially with girls gawking at him. He picked up his drink and took it upstairs. Hopefully, Rita would be at the door of Nelson's Room and would let him in.

She was and she did. He felt less nervous upstairs but wondered if he had made a mistake by coming to the club at all. He wished he had stopped in at Sluggo's for some 'liquid courage,' like the night before. Even in Nelson's Room, it seemed like people were staring at him. He wasn't used to the attention – it felt like they were making fun of him. He wondered if they had noticed he was wearing the same clothes as last night, as the ones he had been photographed in. Once he got a job, he'd have to buy some new clothes, fancy ones, like everyone else.

He ordered his usual drink - a screwdriver - and struck up a conversation with the bartender. He had heard him talking to other customers and thought he had a California accent. Blake asked if he was from the West Coast.

"Not exactly," he answered. "I'm from Phoenix. Horrible place."

Blake laughed and started to tell him about Ridgecrest: "If you think Phoenix is bad, you should visit Ridgecrest…"

"Greyhound?" the bartender asked.

"Greyhound." Blake confirmed.

They had both got to New York the same way – by a Greyhound bus. Most Americans travelled by domestic flights. Only 'poor people' took Greyhounds anymore.

The bartender put out his hand. "I'm Cameron."

"I'm Blake. Blake Webster."

"There's even worse places in Arizona," Cameron said in response to Blake's Ridgecrest stories. You must have gone through Arizona on the coach - did you ever see any billboards on the freeway advertising something called 'The Thing?'"

"Oh yeah! There were tons of them. What is 'The Thing'?"

"Not much. An old farmer converted his farm into a museum where people pay to see weird desert animals in cages - snakes and horny toads and things like that. You see the huge billboards announcing, "man's deadliest enemy," and it draws you in. But when you get there, there's just a barn with some cages in it. Man's deadliest enemy - the 'thing' - is a big spider in a glass case."

Blake laughed. He really wanted to visit the 'museum' when he saw the billboards, but his bus didn't stop near it. He liked Cameron. He wondered how he had got his job at Blunt. Blake wouldn't mind working there.

"Hey, how did you get this job?" he asked. "What did you do before this?"

"Well, to be honest - I'm straight right - but when I first got here, I was starving, I needed money bad - so I worked the area around Times Square. I let gay guys suck me off for $50. Sometimes more. One of them was Howie, the guy who owns this club. He offered me a job."

"Oh," Blake said. Maybe it wasn't such a great job after all. "Those days must have been tough."

Cameron shrugged his shoulders. "It wasn't that bad. If you do something long enough, you sort of get used to it. There was no way I was going to go back to Arizona. I had a bad upbringing. My mother left my father when I was a kid, and he didn't give a fuck about me."

Blake nodded. "I know what you mean." Cameron could tell from the expression on Blake's face that his childhood had probably been as fucked-up as his own. As a bartender, Cameron met a lot of people who had moved to New York to escape their families. They created new families in the city with all the other lost souls.

When Blake finished his drink, Cameron gave him another on the house: "Save your drink tickets, my friend. Here's a 'vodka and air.'"

Blake laughed, took the drink and held it up in a toast. Cameron grabbed his own 'vodka and air' from under the bar - a drink that a customer had left earlier - and clinked Blake's glass - "Waste not, want not."

"Where are you staying, buddy?" Cameron asked.

"Near Times Square. In the Broadway Hotel."

"Ah, yes. The Broadway. I know it well. Is Carl, I mean Carlotta, still working there?"

"Yeah, but why did you call her Carl?"

"She used to be a man called Carl. She had an operation a couple a years ago. One of the resident gangsters paid for it. The hotel is a front for organised crime. The mafia or something. It's a convenient hideaway when one of their guys gets in trouble. One of the heavies fell in love with Carl who was already dressing like a woman. She was getting steroids from some uptown doctor who was into black guys with big boobs. Then, when she got involved with the bank robber, or whatever he was, he did a job and paid for her to have the whole shebang. Carl became Carlotta. She thinks she's important because her boyfriend is 'in' with the guys who own the joint."

"Wow. That's crazy. Is the hotel safe? I'm booked in there for two weeks."

"Probably the safest place in Manhattan. Who's gonna rob a hotel full of gangsters?"

Blake laughed. "Who's Jonesy? Carlotta was arguing with him when I first came in."

"Oh, don't worry about him. He's not a gangster - he's a real tenant. He's more important than he realises. They need real people on welfare in there to add authenticity. She gets a percentage of the rent, so she was probably pissed off she wasn't getting her percentage."

"Hey, Blake, there you are!" It was Phil. "Do you want a line?" he asked, before being interrupted by somebody else tugging at his sleeve. "Hold on a sec," he said and disappeared again.

While Phil was sorting out his customer and Cameron was serving some new customers at the bar, a long-haired guy walked up to Blake and asked him if he was a model. Another person asking him if he was a model; nobody had asked him that in Crumville. He had seen the guy looking at him last night at the club and wondered if he was trying to hit on him.

"No, I'm not a model. Also, I don't mean to be rude but I'm not gay either."

"Don't worry. I am gay, but I'm not trying to pick you up. In fact, I'd prefer it if you *weren't* gay."

"Why?"

"I'm a fashion photographer. Michael Stevens. You'd be perfect for a shoot we're doing."

Anyone in the fashion world would have recognised the name, but Blake wasn't part of that world – yet.

"How tall are you?" he asked Blake.

"I don't know. About 6 ft. 2, I guess. Or 3."

"Perfect. Here's my card. I'm in the Hamptons this weekend, but can you give me a call on Monday? It's my card from *Vogue* but these photos are for *Bellissima*. Here, I'll write my personal number on the other side. But, please, don't give it to anyone."

"Oh. Okay. Thanks."

That was it. As quickly as Michael appeared, he disappeared back into the general melee of the club.

"That guy is really hot right now – he's a fashion photographer. What did he say to you?"

It was Phil. He had sorted out his "friend" in the men's room and had noticed Michael talking to Phil on his way to the bar.

"Really?"

"Yeah. What did he want?"

"He wanted me to be in a photoshoot or something. I'm supposed to call him on Monday. What exactly is a photoshoot?"

"You're joking. It's a... How do you explain a photoshoot? It's a session with a photographer for a magazine. The pictures appear in a fashion magazine. If they're part of an article, that's called 'editorial.' If they're for an ad, it's called 'commercial.' Did he say whether it was editorial or commercial? Commercial is where the money is."

"He just said it was for an Italian magazine. *Belli* something."

"It's probably editorial. But still, it's a beginning. You're tall enough to do the shows.

"What shows?"

"The fashion shows. Haute couture."

"What's that?"

"I can't believe you don't know this. There's either "haute couture" or "ready-to-wear." Haute couture means "high fashion" - limited edition stuff. "Ready-to-wear" is what most of the chicks at this club wear. It's still expensive, but it's 'off the rack' - already made. Like what they sell at department stores. I'm actually wearing a pair of Versace jeans at the moment - ready-to-wear."

He turned around and showed Blake the back pocket of the jeans with a big Medusa label.

"What the hell is that?" Blake asked.

"Versace for god's sakes. These jeans would have cost more than $500 if I had paid for them."

"You stole them.?"

"Susan did."

"Who's Susan?"

"My girlfriend. She doesn't like going out. She says she's still recovering from the last decade of going out. She just sits at home all night, nodding off and watching crap TV. She's strung out on smack."

"Smack?"

"Heroin. It's not a big deal. I do it sometimes to come down from the coke - everybody does - but I'm not strung out like her. She'll do anything for a hit. It's a hassle because most of my profit from the coke goes to support her habit - at least it feels like that sometimes. I have to get her stuff from a place called the Hole in The Wall,' not from my coke supplier, so I have to pay the same price for it that everyone else does."

Blake felt like Phil was talking in a different language. "You shouldn't steal," he said.

"Why not? What's wrong with living a little? What you were putting up your nose last night wasn't exactly legal, was it?

Speaking of which, do you have any of those drink tickets left? Do you wanna do a trade like last time?"

"Yeah, okay. Whiskey again?"

Blake ordered the drinks from Cameron who had overheard their conversation. As Blake left the bar to follow Phil into the men's room, he grabbed Blake's arm: "Watch out for him," he warned about Phil. "He's dangerous."

Blake didn't know what to think. Another warning. Sluggo had warned him about Johnny. He wondered what people thought of him. He wasn't stupid. You had to watch out for yourself in Crumville as well - maybe even more so. People were always trying to steal things at Walt's Mart. He didn't need any more warnings. He could take care of himself. 'Just because I come from a hick town doesn't mean I'm a hick,' he told himself.

Numerous drinks later and who knows how many lines of coke, Blake changed from a small-town shy guy to the type of loud drunk that people avoid at the bar. He kept on grabbing strangers and telling them how great New York was compared to Crumville. They didn't know what he was talking about. Cameron looked worried. He didn't want to have to kick him out of the room.

Phil noticed what was happening and took his friend aside: "C'mon," he said, "it's time for some down time." They went into the men's room and Phil laid out two lines.

"I don't think I can do anymore," Blake said.

"This isn't coke. It will help you to come down."

Blake did the line. He didn't feel anything at first - none of the numbness that he felt when he did coke. But then, suddenly, it was like he'd been hit with a sledgehammer.

"What was that?" he slurred, barely able to keep his eyes open.

"Heroin."

"Heroin!"

"Yeah, don't worry about it. It will help you chill. You're too hyped up from the coke."

Although it was a small line, it hit Blake hard. He had never tried it before and couldn't understand why anyone would. He weaved his way through Nelson's Room, holding onto anything he could for support, until he collapsed at the first empty table he could find. He stayed there the rest of the evening.

"Got any more of those tickets?" Phil asked.

"Yeah, but there's no way I can get to the bar."

"Don't worry, I'll get them."

Phil took the drink tickets to the bar where Cameron served him. He'd been watching them and saw how out of it Blake was. It pissed him off that Phil was taking advantage of Blake. Every time he served Phil, he gave him a dirty look. Phil gave him a dirty look right back and handed over a couple more drink tickets.

"Take care of your friend," he said to Phil.

"I am."

7. The Photoshoot

Saturday morning's hangover was even worse than Friday's. Blake woke up in bed, still in his clothes from last night. He couldn't remember a lot of what happened but what he did remember, embarrassed him. He'd never be able to go back to that club again. He reached into his back pocket to make sure his wallet was still there, and Michael Steven's card fell out. He put it on the bedside table to remind him to call him on Monday. He had to find a job.

He spent most of the day in bed with a headache. At one point he got a takeaway at Gigi's - another ham and cheese panini and a strong coffee. Luigi laughed when he saw him. "You look like a corpse," he said. That's what he felt like. A corpse. After he ate the sandwich and drank the coffee, he went back to bed. When he woke up, it was already dark out. He had slept most of the day.

He wondered what he was going to do if he didn't go to the club. It was a Saturday night. There was always Sluggo's, but he would have to pay for his drinks there - at least some of them. Maybe nobody at the club had seen him nodding off last night. The table where he and Phil were sitting was in a dark corner. Howie wasn't even at the club. Phil hadn't mentioned his brief conversation with Cameron.

By 11 pm, Blake was standing outside Blunt again, trying to get Howie's attention. Howie waved him in: "You don't have to stand with the crowd, Blake. Just come up to the rope. Eloise will let you in."

Another night at Blunt began. Phil was also there, of course, but this time they stuck to booze and cocaine. Every time Cameron served them, he did what he did on Friday night. He gave Phil a dirty look. Phil ignored him this time. He didn't want Blake to see.

When Blake woke up the next day and realised it was Sunday, he was relieved. Sunday was a day of rest. There was no way that he'd be going to Blunt on a Sunday night. Was it even open on a Sunday night? He spent most of the day looking for jobs on his laptop. When he saw the same companies advertising the same jobs that they had been advertising since Thursday, he started to get worried. Maybe the listings were for jobs that didn't exist. Maybe he needed to scour the streets for physical, 'help wanted' signs. He promised himself he would do that on Monday, after a day of rest today, Sunday.

By 10 pm he was at Sluggo's and by 11 at Blunt. They let him in free, but Howie and Eloise weren't there, so he wasn't given any drink tickets. He bought a drink in Nelson's room and waited for Phil to arrive. They did a couple of lines in the men's room, but the evening fizzled out early. He was in bed by 2 am, about two hours earlier than the previous nights.

On Monday morning, he rang Michael Stevens on the number on the back of his card. He had promised he would call and maybe Michael would know of a job. He practiced what he was going to say in advance - that he was willing to do almost anything, that he was skinny but strong – he had lifted heavy boxes at Walt's Mart - and he could do mathematics - he had been responsible for the yearly inventory at the store.

He dialled the number Michael had given him and nervously waited for someone to answer. It rang and rang and rang. Finally, a male voice said. "Hello?"

He recognised Michael's voice and nearly hung up. He instantly forgot everything he planned to say.

"Is that Mr. Stevens?" he asked.

"Yes, this is Michael. Who is that?"

Blake could hear a lot of music in the background. Michael sounded angry, like Blake had interrupted a party. What a mistake this was. He felt like a fool. Michael probably wouldn't even remember him. Who knows how many people he gave his card to that night?

"It's Blake. Blake Webster. I met you..."

"Blake! Wow! What a coincidence. I'm so glad that you called. I'm at the studio now. Listen, is there any way you could get here right away? We had another model booked for today - a new guy called José but he didn't show up. He's not answering his phone. The agency said they'd continue to ring him, but I told them not to bother. They offered to send someone else, but I need your blue eyes."

"You want me to come down now? Yeah. Of course, I can. Where are you?"

"In a studio on 36th and 10th"

"I'm on 40th and 9th. I'll be there in ten minutes."

"You're a lifesaver. I can't guarantee anything - I don't know how you'll photograph - I can give you $100 for showing up and another $400 if you work out. Would that be okay?"

Okay? Blake would have done it for free, just to meet some new people. He liked Phil but wanted to meet normal people; ones who weren't so druggy.

"Yeah, that's okay. I'll be right down. What should I wear? I don't have many clothes with me. Is there a dress code?"

"Dress code? It's a studio Blake, not a club. Wear what you've got on. We have tons of clothes here."

"Okay. I'll be right there."

"Listen, since you're so close, would you mind stopping off at Gigi's on your way here - it's at 38th and 9th. An Italian coffee shop. Can you get me a double macchiato with extra foam on top?

"Yeah, of course, I know the place. A double what?"

Michael laughed. "It's a coffee. A double macchiato. Ask them for extra foam. Tell them its's for Michael Stevens. They know me. Get one for yourself as well. And some croissants. I'll give you the money when you get here. "Wait a second. Does anyone else want a coffee?" he yelled out to the other people on the shoot - his assistant, the models, the stylist and the hair and make-up artists. Of course, everyone did. "Sorry to lay this on you, but I've got quite an order here." He reeled off a list of coffees of every type, croissants and a *pain* of this and a *pain* of that - *pain* meaning bread in French, Blake learned. He couldn't figure out why an Italian diner was selling French bread, but he was happy to get whatever they wanted.

"Can you manage it?" Michael asked when he was finished.

"Yes, of course I can. I'll be right there."

Blake grabbed his coat and a piece of paper he had written everyone's order on. Luigi was happy to see him and especially happy to see the large order he had. "Are you working for Slick now?" he asked.

"No, not really. Well sort of. A photographer who works for them wants me to be in a photo-shoot and he asked me to get them some coffees on the way."

As Luigi helped one of the sandwich guys with the order, he silently congratulated himself on being right about Blake when he first walked into the diner. He had known then that he would make something of himself - unlike that loser nephew of his, Phil. As soon as Blake left with the sandwiches, Luigi went into the office and rang Phil - "So Blake's working for Slick now..." he said, rubbing it in. He could hear Susan complaining on the other side of the bed: "There's nothing left. Who did the cotton?"

"Get rid of that girl, Phil. She's trouble. For all of us. Tell her to shove her cotton up her ass." Luigi wasn't stupid. He knew that junkies used a small bit of cotton - usually a cigarette filter - to filter their dope before drawing it up into the syringe after cooking it. He heard Phil put the phone down, the sound of a slap and then, the sound of Susan crying.

"You shouldn't hit girls," Luigi said, playing the responsible uncle, but he didn't really give a shit about how Phil treated Susan. He just wanted her out of the picture. Junkies were bad news. They attracted too much attention from the police.

Cocaine was a different story, altogether. "What time are you going to be around today for the pick-up?" Phil asked.

"Not on the fucking phone, Phil! How many times do I have to tell you! I don't even know what you mean by pick up. You mean pick up your lunch?"

"Yeah. My lunch. What time do I pick up my lunch?"

"Whenever you fucking want, you idiot."

Luigi hung up the phone. If Phil wasn't his nephew, Luigi's bosses would probably have got rid of him a long time ago. As a small-time dealer, Phil wasn't that important. He could be replaced easily. The only thing that kept him from being an "expendable" – someone whose life could easily be sacrificed for the greater good (or evil) – was the fact that he was Luigi's nephew. Something had to be done about Susan, though. She was trouble. He wondered how long she would last.

The studio wasn't far from Luigi's. When Blake arrived with the coffees, he instantly became everyone's best friend. First, they rushed to get their coffees. Then they noticed the person delivering them.

"OMG Michael!" one of the female models said. "Where did you find him? He's gorgeous."

Michael's male photo assistant said, "He's hot. Is he straight or gay?"

"Straight," Michael answered. The assistant looked disappointed.

"Dibs!" another model joked, leaning her head on his shoulder. She explained to Blake, "Most of the good-looking guys in New York are gay." He laughed, enjoying the attention.

He was the only male model in the shoot. The rest were women and they all had blue eyes. That was the theme of the shoot - "Blue" - which seemed to be the colour of the moment.

Didn't everyone feel "blue" in the winter?

There wasn't much of a set. Most of it would be photoshopped in later. Stevens wanted the pictures to look like they were shot through a peephole, like Marcel Duchamp's Étant donnés. He had come across it in a book of Duchamp's art at the home of a guy he had picked up at Uncle Larry's, a gay bar in Greenwich Village.

"C'mon girls, drink up! We've got work to do and we're running late." Michael shouted. "Here Blake, sit here," he said, pointing to a metal folding chair. I'll get Gable to do your make up. Paul Gable was a big make-up artist in the industry - both in statue and size. Most heroin addicts were skinny, but Paul had a raging habit and was still overweight. Very overweight. Everyone knew he was a heroin addict, but he was so good at his job, nobody cared how small his pupils were.

"Make-up?" Blake asked. He didn't know he'd be wearing make-up. He looked at the amount of make-up Paul was wearing and became concerned.

"Yes, make-up," Paul said. "Don't worry, 'dahling.' It's just to make you look like you already do. Meanwhile Mitzi will sort out the clothes."

Mitzi was one of the best stylists in the business. She had managed to get some of the most important designers in New York to lend her clothes for the shoot. It was "editorial", but they would get a mention in the credits. So would the photographer, make-up artist and stylist. Not the models though. They rarely got a credit. Blake didn't mind about the credit, he was just glad that he had a job, even if it was only for a day.

Modelling came easy for Blake, mostly because he didn't know what he was doing. He just followed Michael's directions: "Turn your head that way, look up, look down, smile, don't smile, look at the model, look behind me..." Because he wasn't trying to 'model,' he made the perfect model. He let the camera find him, and the camera loved what it found.

About an hour into the shoot, the buzzer went on the studio door. Michael hated being interrupted in the middle of a shoot. Blake was doing so well, that he hoped it wasn't the missing model. His assistant went to the door and came back with a middle-aged woman who looked anything but fashionable. People in the business joked that she went for the "anti-fashion" look although one particularly bitchy hair stylist called it the "doesn't care how she looks" look. Not to her face, of course.

Nobody would dare insult Ava to her face.

"Ava!" Michael exclaimed. "How delightful," he lied, as he kissed her on both cheeks.

"Who is she?" Blake whispered to another model.

"Ava. She's head of the men's division."

"*Her*?" Blake asked, surprised.

The model held her finger to her mouth - "Shhh..."

Blake thought "Ava" was such a glamorous name – wasn't there an old actress named Ava something or other? There was nothing glamorous about the woman he was looking at. Ava didn't give a damn about her appearance. She wasn't into fashion; she was into money. She'd been wearing the same dress for so many years that it was almost back in style; a black caftan that (she thought) hid her bulges, but all it really did was accentuate the black circles under her eyes. Sleep wasn't her thing. She had a reputation for being as hard as nails but could also be surprisingly sweet when she had to - like now when she had to apologise about José not showing up.

"I'm not sure what happened." she said. "We're still trying to find him. Maybe he went back to the Canaries. He's new. He was scouted by one of our guys on holiday. He was sunbathing in an area called "the dunes," or something like that. At night he worked at a bar at someplace called the "Yumbo." He lived with his grandmother in the Playa de Ingles. I might have some of that wrong – I need to check his bio – but he seemed dependable. We used him for several jobs, and he always showed up on time."

"The dunes!?" Michael blurted.

The dunes were a gay cruising ground; sandy hills that led to the beach which provided cover under the daytime sun for all sorts of sexual going-ons. Ava's mention of them inspired Michael's assistant to share a story about how he got lost in them on one visit to the Canaries. He was stoned on acid at the time. He spent most of the afternoon trying to find his way back to his hotel which turned out to be only a few minutes away. All the dunes looked so similar that he had been going around in circles, hallucinating.

"I didn't mind that much." he said. "I'd be walking around in the middle of nothingness and then suddenly come across a naked guy fisting someone..."

Ava looked uncomfortable and turned back to Michael, "Anyway, Michael, I'm very sorry about José. It won't happen again."

"Don't worry Ava. Blake is working out like a dream. I'm actually glad that José didn't show. Blake is better."

He might as well have stabbed her in her purse. Michael was one of the few photographers in New York who could set his own terms. His contract with Slick was non-exclusive which meant that if he wasn't satisfied with the models or service he received, he was free to work for someone else and Slick would lose out on its 30% commission. And, of course, if he used a model not signed to Slick, they'd lose their model's commission too. She could kill José for not showing up and murder Blake for being so good. Blake wasn't signed to them. They wouldn't get a commission.

"I'm so sorry," Ava said, with as much sincerity she could muster, given the situation.

"There's nothing to be sorry about," Michael reassured her. "Blake is better. Everything is fine."

"I'm so glad it worked out so well," she lied. "I just wanted to say sorry."

"Thanks Ava, but we better get back to work."

"Michael, can you send me some of the photographs you've already done, so I can have a look at them on my way back to the office?"

Michael grunted. He hated sending out raw photographs, before the background was inserted, but she was the boss and he had to do what she said. He sent a selection of shots directly from his camera and continued with the shoot. Ava looked at them on her phone and stayed another ten minutes, watching the session from the studio door. 'Any idiot could see how good-looking Blake was,' she thought, but she also wanted to see how he moved, how he took direction, and how he got on with the other models. All she needed was ten minutes to be impressed.

After she left, Michael said, "That was weird."

"What was?" Blake asked. He wondered if somebody had complained about him. Maybe he was having too much fun. Modelling didn't feel like work.

"It's not unusual for someone from the agency to show up, but I've never known Ava to come, herself."

"Did I do something wrong?" Blake asked worried.

"Not as far as I'm concerned. You're doing great. Let's keep on working."

Ava walked back to her office, too angry to wait for a cab,

cursing José all the way. She looked again at the pictures from Michael on her phone. He was right about Blake. He was better than José. Much better.

When she got back to Slick, she went straight to the Legal Department and asked for a copy of José's contract. She wanted to make sure she could fire him without having to pay him off. She'd keep him on the books at the moment – he still had some jobs booked for the future - but she wanted to know what the legal situation was, just in case. She also asked the lawyers to draft a new contract for "Blake Webster" and get it to her office as soon as possible.

After seeing the lawyers, she went to her office, without saying a word to her secretary as she passed through the reception area. She unlocked the top drawer of her desk and took out a small mirror with two lines of coke on it. She allowed herself three lines a day and had already done her morning line. She looked at her watch and saw that it wasn't even noon yet. She didn't care. She did her lunchtime line anyway. Then she looked at her watch again. She loved that watch. A gold Cartier Tank. She might not spend much on clothes, but she didn't skimp on jewellery. She'd much rather have an expensive watch than an expensive family.

She stared at the watch - or at least the name "Cartier" - as the cocaine worked its way into her system. She loved how numb it made her feel. She once had a much larger habit but had managed to cut it down to three lines a day. She had started buying it from Phil, but when she found out he was getting it from Luigi, she went straight to the source. It meant she could avoid Phil who she thought was unbearably sleazy. Phil wasn't happy – he didn't get his cut anymore – but it was much more convenient for Ava, and the quality was better. All she had to do was to call Luigi at the restaurant and tell him she needed "extra sugar" with her coffee delivery that day.

Her habit got out of control after that. It was too easy to get the stuff. She ended up going to Narcotics Anonymous, but she didn't feel comfortable in an environment that required so much honesty. She wasn't about to air her dirty laundry in public. NA's slogan of "What you hear here, let it stay here," was bullshit, as far as she was concerned. The fashion world revolved on gossip, and she simply could not believe that what was heard at meetings would not end up elsewhere. She stopped going to meetings and managed to limit herself to three lines a day through sheer willpower. At least that's what she thought she was doing. After her first line of the morning, she usually couldn't stop thinking about the next one and often dipped into her "emergency supply" which she kept in a small Gucci wallet on the top shelf of her office cupboard behind a stack of files she never used, marked "PRIVATE." She never shared her stash and when people offered her a line at a social event, she always said "no." It wasn't easy, but at least everyone thought she was "clean."

8. The Hit

After the photo-session, Blake went straight to Sluggo's. He didn't even stop at his hotel to put his money away. Michael had given him $500 in cash as his fee.

"I'm famous!" he announced as he threw a stack of cash on the bar. "Drinks for everyone in the house!"

The "house" at that time consisted of himself, Sluggo and Johnny the junkie dribbling in the corner. Maybe one or two others. In the permanent darkness of the place, it was difficult to tell whether there were human beings in the overcoats at the other end of the room.

Sluggo stared at the money like an alien had just landed. "What the hell?" he asked with raised eyebrows.

Blake laughed and explained about the modelling job. He put most of the cash back in his pocket, leaving a few twenties on the bar to pay for the drinks.

The mention of money woke Johnny up from his nod. He was at the bar in a flash. He asked if he could have cash instead of a drink and Blake handed him a twenty. "Don't spend it all in one place," he yelled after Johnny who was already out the door looking for a connection who could score for him. He wasn't allowed at the place where Phil got his girlfriend's stuff - the Hole in The Wall - because he had tried to kick the door in once when they wouldn't give him credit.

Blake spent a couple of hours at Sluggo's, telling him and whoever else would listen about all the fun that afternoon. At one point a young couple came in who weren't much older than Blake and started to leave as soon as they got a look at the place. They stayed when Blake offered to buy them a drink. They were visiting from New Jersey and had just seen a Broadway show. They loved hearing about his photo-session. They had some coke on them and treated him to a line in the bathroom. Sluggo wasn't happy when they got back to the bar.

"You're getting out of control Blake. No drugs. Do you understand me? No drugs. The last thing I need is to get busted. I don't care if you're on them, but don't do them here. I don't let Johnny do them here and neither should you. Understand?"

Blake nodded. But he resented the comparison to Johnny. Yes, he had tried drugs with Phil, even heroin once, but he wasn't an addict. He didn't sit in a corner all night dribbling like Johnny did.

"Blake, I like you, but be careful. Don't let New York change you."

That was the second time that Sluggo warned him about New York. He wished people would stop doing that. If they were so worried about New York, why were they still living here?

"Don't worry, I'm not going to change."

"You already have."

Blake didn't know what to say. He hoped he never became as bitter as Sluggo. He apologised about the coke, told him it would never happen again and left for Blunt.

Sluggo felt awful for having been so severe. He wished Blake had stayed longer; that their conversation hadn't ended up like it had. The bar was empty now. He stood there staring at the row of vacant bar stools and wondered when life had stopped being fun.

* * * * *

Howie was standing on his wooden box when Blake arrived at Blunt. One of his model friends had already told him about the photo-session: "You know that guy, Blake, who comes to the club? He was one of the models at Michael's shoot and, get this, he's straight!"

"I didn't know you were straight," he joked with Blake from his soapbox.

"Huh?"

Howie laughed. "Here's some drink tickets, gorgeous. Get in there."

Howie yelled after him, "I heard it was a great photo-session!"

Blake understood now and laughed. "I'll buy you a drink inside!" he shouted, waving the drink tickets that Howie had just given him. Eloise let him know that she had rung Rita in Nelson's Room "to let her know you're on your way," as he entered the club.

As soon as Blake got upstairs, he ran into Phil who also knew about the shoot - both from his uncle and one of the other models who he sold coke to.

"Hey superstar, let's do a line," he said to Blake.

He didn't even ask for a trade. Blake followed him into the

men's room and Phil made two fat lines.

"Everybody's saying how great you were at the photo-session," Phil said just before inhaling a whole line with one nostril.

"Who's everybody?" Blake asked, as Phil handed him the dollar he had used as a straw.

"I don't know. You know. 'Everybody'."

After Blake snorted half a line with each nostril, Phil energetically kicked the cubicle door open like a cowboy kicking a saloon door and said "Let's go!"

When they got to the bar, Blake ordered two drinks and the evening began. Another whirlwind of a night. At the end of it, Phil asked Blake if he wanted to do some of the "special stuff." "Just a little bit," he was quick to add, "to bring us down - I don't have much - it's from Susan's stash."

"Okay, as long as it *is* just a little bit. The last time was too much."

"Don't worry, it won't be like that."

When they got into the cubicle, Phil took out a spoon and a syringe from his inside jacket pocket.

"What's that?"

"Don't worry. You feel it more if you shoot it up. It's such a small amount that we wouldn't feel it at all if we snorted it. You're not afraid of needles, are you?"

"No, of course I'm not afraid of needles."

Phil took a small glassine bag of white powder and his "works" from his inside jacket pocket - a spoon and a plastic syringe - and ripped off the filter from an unsmoked cigarette to use as a "cotton." From his outer jacket pocket, he took a small plastic bottle of water that had been there all night. He showed Blake how to mix the powder with the water in the spoon and to "cook" it with a lighter to make sure all the powder had dissolved. He then drew it up into the plunger of the syringe, through the cotton to filter out any undissolved bits that had gone unnoticed. He tied his belt around his upper arm to make his veins stand out and, after tapping out any air bubbles, he slowly slid the needle into his arm. When he was finished, he handed everything - his "works" - to Blake who stared at him with disbelief.

"What am I supposed to do with this?" he asked.

"Just do what I did. I'll guide you through it. You might as well learn now. I might not be around the next time."

Blake was reticent. He didn't even like the stuff the last time they did it. But he didn't want Phil to think he was a wimp, so he followed his directions and it turned out to be easier than he thought. He didn't feel so bad this time. He just felt relaxed. And happy.

"There," Phil said, "That wasn't so difficult, was it?" If you ever need some disposable syringes, there's a drug store in Times Square that will sell them to you if you say you're a diabetic. Or you can use a needle exchange - just check the web."

Blake strongly doubted that he would ever need to use a needle exchange. Or a package of syringes. Although the dope felt better this time, he had no intention of making it a habit.

9. Mr. Wang's

Blake felt worse when he woke up the next morning than on any of the previous mornings. His mouth felt like sandpaper, and his body ached like he was coming down with a cold. And there was that damn phone again. Did it ever stop ringing? Next time, he was going to put it on silent. Or at least change the ringtone from "techno bleep."

Phil and he hadn't drunk as much as usual - he still had drink tickets left at the end of the night - but he still felt like shit. After their hit, they chilled at one of the tables talking like old friends. Blake told Phil about his childhood, his father, his father's safe and his mother. Phil mostly talked about his girlfriend. He had met her when she was working at a strip joint in New Jersey he used to go to. The Jersey strip joints were better than the New York ones because the rules weren't so strict; at least nobody followed them. Most were fronts for whorehouses. Phil liked blondes with big tits. Susan certainly fit the bill, but Blake wondered how much of her was real. Phil couldn't care less. He'd have sex with an inflatable doll if he had the chance.

Sometimes one of his Phil's customers would come to the table, but he said that he didn't have anything; that he was just chilling with his friend, Blake, who had just done a big photo-session for Slick. A few of the models from the session came up to say hello. They didn't even want any coke, they just wanted to say hi to Blake. Phil felt like he was sitting with fashion's next superstar. The only person who didn't know he was a superstar was Blake.

The "techno bleep" continued as Blake thought about last night. He wished he hadn't yapped so much about his childhood.

"Damn that phone! He still felt spaced out from the smack last night and would have liked to stay in bed. He found the phone tangled up in his bedspread and answered it, thinking it might be Phil wanting to meet for a strong coffee.

"Blake! Sorry to bother you - Michael gave me your number."

He recognised the voice and hoped that his didn't sound too rough when he asked "Ava?" He thought he could hear the sound of a drawer closing on her end before she answered.

"Yes, darling, it's little ole' me," she answered sweetly. "I hope I didn't wake you."

"No, of course not," he croaked feebly. He looked at his phone. It was 11.00.

"You're not burning the candles at both ends already, are you, darling? You know the expression: 'early to bed early to rise, makes a man healthy, wealthy and wise.'"

"Yes, of course." It sounded like something his father would say.

"I've had a look at your photographs, Blake. And they really are fabulous."

"Gee thanks. That's very nice of you."

"So what time are you letting me take you out to lunch today?"

"Well, to be honest, I would love to have lunch with you, I really would, but I have to look for a job. You see, I've been here almost a week now and I haven't had a single interview."

There was a pause as she absorbed what he said in astonishment. Surely, he must realise that lunch with her might result in a job. "What sort of job were you looking for sweetheart?"

"I don't know. Maybe a waiter or something like that."

"How unique. My driver will pick you up at 1:00. Is Chinese food okay?"

As it was Chinese food, which he assumed wouldn't cost very much, he took her up on her offer, unaware that Mr. Wang's was one of the most expensive celebrity-laden restaurants in New York.

"I'm transferring you to my secretary. She'll get your details. Will see you later."

There was a click and then a different woman was on the phone, asking where she should send the car. The last thing he wanted was a car pulling up in front of the dump he was staying in. He asked for the address of the restaurant and said he would meet Ava there.

"The address? It's Mr. Wang's. I don't know the address. Ava said to send a car for you. She'll be upset if I don't do what she says."

"Um, ok, tell the driver to pick me up in front of the Empire State Building." It was the only building he was familiar with, apart from Blunt.

"The what?"

"The Empire State Building."

"You're staying in the Empire State Building?"

"No, but I'll be outside it at 1. I promise. Sorry I've got to go." He didn't actually have to go, but he was afraid she'd ask more questions that he wouldn't be able to answer.

Ava's secretary hung the phone up slowly, as if she hadn't understood the conversation. Ava was standing next to her. She had come out of her office to listen in on the call.

"What's the matter?" she asked.

"He said to send the car to the Empire State Building. Where is the Empire State Building?"

"How should I know?" Having spent her entire adult life in Manhattan, she had passed it numerous times but couldn't remember what street it was on. She looked out the window. "There, isn't that it?"

"No, that's the Chrysler Building."

"Don't worry, the driver will know."

Ava went back to her office and tried to resist opening her top drawer again. Only one line was left. 'Oh fuck it,' she thought as she helped herself to it. She would dip into her emergency supply later if she needed to. If that ran out, she could always call Luigi to get a coffee with "extra sugar" delivered.

* * * * *

When Ava arrived at Wang's that afternoon, she was whisked upstairs to her usual table in the darkened VIP section by Charles, the maître d'. As she slipped him a twenty-dollar bill on the way to the table, he whispered that her guest had already arrived. Blake stood up when he saw her, looking uncomfortable in his flannel shirt and faded blue jeans. He thought the restaurant would be like the cheap Chinese restaurants in Crumville, but everyone was dressed up and looked much more important than him. The first thing he did when him and Ava sat down was to apologise for what he was wearing.

"Blake, please don't worry about that," she reassured him," although your naivety is absolutely charming. Have you never heard the expression, 'the meek shall inherit the earth?'"

He had heard it but didn't know what it meant. She knew what it meant but had never bothered to follow it.

"Shall I order for both of us?" she asked, as she ordered for both of them. "The soft-shell crabs are dynamite."

"Yeah, that would be good," he said. He had no idea what

they were, but he didn't want her to think he was stupid.

"What about wine?" she asked. "Would you like a glass? I tend to stick with water, myself, during lunch."

"Water is fine with me," he lied. He could do with a glass of wine, but it would probably cost a fortune in a place like this. Ava was relieved. The last thing she needed on her books was another alcoholic or drug addict. Clean-living Blake was an agency's dream.

When she was finished ordering, he whispered to her, "I don't know how to use chopsticks."

She yelled out to the departing waiter, "And can we have some silverware for my friend? He doesn't know how to use chopsticks."

If Blake hadn't already felt like he was dying from a hangover, he probably would have died from embarrassment.

The waiter turned to Ava and bowed: "Of course, Madam."

Ava turned to Blake and said: "First of all thank you helping us out with that photo-session on such late notice. That was really appreciated and noted for the future. But that's not why I'm here now – well not directly anyway. A well-known brand of men's grooming products has contacted us. They've asked us to send some models to a 'go see.' Do you know what that is?"

"No, can't say I do."

"It's an appointment where a client checks the models out. It's more like a 'go and get checked out' appointment than a 'going' and 'seeing.' There'll be models there from other agencies too. They'll photograph the ones they like and show the photos to their art directors, company bosses - whoever. Then they'll call back the models they want to be photographed by their own photographer. Eventually they make a decision. Sometimes the process can go on forever."

"I suppose I can do it, but I'll have to work the appointments around whatever job I get. Is that okay?"

"What job?"

"I told you, I need to get a job. There's no way I'm going back to Ridgecrest."

"What's Ridgecrest?"

"It's where I'm from. I thought I told you before. It used to be called Crumville."

"Don't worry, darling, regardless of what happens, we're not going to send you back to Crumville. The company is looking for new faces that haven't already been plastered all over New

York. They're looking for Mr. Average except the real Mr. Average is an unshaven middle-aged pig. So, we have to give them a gorgeous Mr. Average – the Mr. Average that every Mr. Average would like to be. Someone like you."

"Well, I guess I'm pretty average but I'm not so sure about the gorgeous part."

"Exactly what I mean!" she nearly shouted. "Only Mr. Average would say something like that. You really are perfect."

"What do I have to do?"

"The main thing is to show up. That's a very big part of modelling. Showing up. If they call you back, you'll have to show up again."

"And that's it?"

"Well, it depends on what happens. There'll be other models there from other agencies. If it was up to me, I would certainly choose you for the job, but it's not up to me – although I will make it known that I think you're perfect. The company is called Style Raven. They make things like shaving cream, men's hair gel, that sort of thing. Are you interested?"

"Well, I guess so..."

She could tell something was bothering him. "What is it, Blake? I can tell something is up. It's a sense I have. That's how I got to the top of the ladder."

Ava might have a "sixth sense" about some things, but it wasn't what got her to the "top of the ladder." Slick had been started by her mother who had previously managed another agency. She put her daughter, Ava, in charge of the Men's Division. She remained in that position after her mother sold the agency to a large conglomerate. Although Ava had fought battles through the years to retain her position, she had initially got her foot in the door because of her genes.

"It sounds like a long process, and I need a job now."

"Don't worry, I'm coming to that. We need you to join the agency in order to put you forward for the job. Would you be willing to do that? Would you like to become part of our little family?" Hopefully, Blake didn't notice the dollar signs in her eyes. Even if he didn't get the Style Raven job, Michael Stevens wanted to use him for future campaigns.

"Yeah, of course I would," Blake said with the gratitude of an orphan who had just been placed with a loving family. He didn't know it at the time, but the Slick "family" was neither small nor particularly loving. They employed more than three thousand people in six different countries, and you were only part of the "family" as long as you generated income for them. A model's contract could be terminated at any time for any reason by them, but the model wasn't allowed to cancel it, themselves - at least not without paying a hefty fee and a percentage of future earnings. Even for a modelling agency, their standard contract was ruthless. There were so many terms and conditions that most of the models they "discovered" just signed on the dotted line without reading them. It didn't make that much difference. One of the terms and conditions was that the terms and conditions could be changed by the agency at any time.

Ava continued: "If you do join, I'll put you on a retainer until the Style Raven decision comes through. Even if you don't get that job, I'm sure there'll be other work. You'd only be able to work for us, of course, although other agencies could borrow you at our discretion, and of course we would get our percentage for those jobs too. I've got a copy of a contract in my bag, if you'd like to see it. It's pretty standard stuff."

She pulled out a twenty-page contact and handed it to him. He quickly turned to the final page. He wasn't a very good reader but didn't want to tell her that. When he started to sign it, she pretended to try to stop him.

"Blake are you sure you don't want to have a lawyer look at that before you sign it? I can't stress that enough."

Blake didn't have a lawyer: "I trust you, Ava. Everyone from Slick has been so nice to me."

He thought about all the fun they had during the photo-session. He loved New York. Anything could happen. One day he was a nobody and the next day he was signing a contract to be a model, just like in the movies. He handed the signed document back to Ava. She couldn't get it into her bag fast enough.

"Oh Blake, you have no idea how happy you've made me. You really have. It will be wonderful to have you as part of our little family. I know that neither of us our drinkers, but I think we should celebrate. They have champagne by the glass here. I'm going to order two. Is that okay?"

Of course, it was okay. He was dying for a drink.

* * * *

Blake hardly saw Ava after joining the Slick "family." Her

secretary rang later that afternoon to tell him the address for the "go see" the next day. The agency had already emailed Perlco, who owned the Style Raven brand, with photos from his first and only photo-session and a personal message from Ava recommending her new find: "He's everything the boy next door would like to be."

The process of finding the new face of Style Raven was quicker than anyone at Slick expected once the executives at Perlco got a look at Blake. They thought he was perfect. After a few test sessions with their photographer, they thought he was even more perfect.

Ava negotiated a tough contract with them. Blake would be paid an initial retainer of $100,000, plus a promise of considerable royalties on the sale of every can of shaving cream, tube of hair gel and bottle of after-shave that his image appeared on. He was free to do editorial work, providing that Style Raven products were used and credited (or at least credited), but he wasn't allowed to appear on any other company's ads. Slick, as per their standard contract, would get 30% of everything that Blake got. By the weekend he was in a photographer's studio doing his first shoot for the brand. His Style Raven career had begun.

Perlco held a big party in Nelson's Room announcing the new face of Style Raven to the media. Phil was there. Blake noticed Ava staring at them when they were at the bar together. She didn't look happy. She made a mental note to tell Blake to choose his friends wisely; she didn't want him to become one of Phil's customers. Models on dope were a hassle. At least she kept her 'occasional' use of cocaine, a secret.

Ava hated PR parties, but it was part of her job. Fortunately, she left early; if she had stayed, she would have seen Phil's girlfriend get kicked out by security. Whenever Phil had talked about Susan in the past, he complained about how she was always on the nod, but she certainly wasn't on the nod at the Style Raven party - just the opposite. She was embarrassingly over-animated, acting like Phil was the guest of honour rather than Blake. It was an open bar; guests could drink as much as they wanted, and she did. Too much. She kept on making a big deal about Phil talking to other girls - mostly his customers from Slick. When she threw a drink at her boyfriend, security got involved. As they led her out of the club, she apologised - "it was the only way I could get his attention" - and promised to behave herself in cutesy baby language. When that didn't work, she spat at them.

"Stupid bitch," Phil shouted at her before another security guy grabbed him and threw him out too. He managed to slip Blake a wrap of "blow" on his way out, which got him through the rest of the evening.

The announcement that Blake was the new face of Style Raven got a lot of space in the fashion press, including the front cover of *Man's World* - a throwaway style magazine for men who would never think of spending money on such a thing, but which could be found in most barber shops of the world. It had a huge circulation. In France it was called *La Monde de l'homme*, in Spain, *Hombre Mundo*. It was while he was waiting for a haircut at his local barber in Ridgecrest that Blake's father saw pictures of his son in the magazine. He had already seen an image that looked like Blake on one of the cans of shaving cream on the counter in the barber's shop, but it had been altered so much that he couldn't be sure it really was his son. His face had been smoothed, his eyes made extra blue and part of his chin was covered in shaving foam.

When John Webster saw the front cover of the magazine, however, and read the article inside, there was no mistaking the fact that his son was now being used to advertise sissy grooming products like tinted moisturiser and coloured lip balm. He grunted with embarrassment. What sort of man wore make-up? He hoped that his barber hadn't noticed. The last thing he wanted was attention drawn to him or his family - or his safe. When town people asked about his son, he told them that he was at college back east.

The longer Blake's father waited for his cut, the angrier he got. He was outraged that his failure of a son who had called him disgusting had turned out to be such a success. He wondered how much money he got by wasting his time posing like that and decided it must be a fortune. John Webster remembered how hard he had worked as an avocado farmer (before he became an oil millionaire by fluke), that he felt insulted by his son's easy success.

'What would that mommy's boy know about work?' he mumbled to himself in the car on his way home. 'Having your picture taken isn't work.' By the time he got to his front door he was fumbling with his keys so much that he could barely open it. As soon as he did, he went straight upstairs to the attic and got out his stash of porn.

John Webster's porn collection had grown considerably since the disappearance of his wife and son. He had to go to specialist shops in Palmdale to get the magazines he craved now. There weren't any stores in Crumville selling magazines with articles that featured sex slaves dressed in rubber who begged to be abused. He especially liked to fantasize about his wife hanging from a noose while he whipped her as she urinated in fear. Sometimes he even tied a noose around his own neck when he jacked himself off. The tightness of the noose made him feel dizzy, like he was drunk. He always came before he lost consciousness and made sure he was standing on a stool so that he wouldn't choke. The magazines called it autoerotic asphyxiation. Sometimes he considered going to Palmdale to find a prostitute who would help him act out his fantasies, but he always chickened out. His stash in the safe had grown considerably since his wife's thievery and the last thing he needed was a nosey neighbour seeing him arrive home with a prostitute.

He spread his stash of porn around the stool in the attic, opened to his current favourite pages. Sitting on the stool, he masturbated furiously, his erotic anger veering from Blake to Blake's mother, his wife, who had deserted him after everything he had done for her. 'The dirty whore,' he groaned as he shot his load.

Usually, he cleaned everything up afterwards but his time he just went to bed exhausted. He was in his early seventies now and sometimes he got so excited during his sessions that he was afraid of having a heart attack.

* * * * *

While Blake's father busied himself in his attic, Blake was busy becoming New York's latest fashion superstar. Everybody wanted a piece of Blake Webster. A production company in Hollywood even put forward a proposal for a documentary on his meteoric rise to fame but Ava nixed it. She planned on making a lot of money from him in the future and didn't want him to peak too soon. Besides, the company's fee was abysmal by fashion industry standards.

The next few months were the busiest in Blake's life and he enjoyed every minute of his new-found fame. In Slick he found a new family and in Phil, the best friend he never had while growing up in Crumville. With the money he made from Style Raven, he was able to move into a luxurious one-bedroom apartment in Chelsea. Slick helped him to find it. They were also one of the owners of the building. Most of the money he made from Slick went back to Slick in one way or another. When they booked him a car, for instance, the cost was deducted from his royalties as a "recoupable expense," as specified in the contract he had signed at Mr. Wang's.

Blake's new apartment wasn't far from Phil and Susan's place. Phil was impressed by how luxurious it was. It was small but there were mirrors and black marble everywhere. Phil hassled him for a set of keys so he could take back girls that that he met at the club, but Blake refused; he didn't feel right enabling his friend to have sex behind his girlfriend's back, regardless of what he thought of Susan. Phil criticised him for his "small town" attitude.

"Everybody does it, for crissakes," he would say.

And Blake would answer, "then get them to do it."

Phil did. All it took was a quarter gram of coke and most of his friends were willing do anything for him, except for Blake. Sometimes it pissed him off.

"Someday, you'll grow up and become a man like the rest of us," Phil would say to Blake. It was the sort of thing Blake's father used to say.

10. José

Once all the Style Raven photos were done and Blake's face was plastered all over town, he had more time to spend with Phil. Although he could still do editorial work, Ava wanted to "keep it in the family." He was generally limited to working with photographers who were also signed to Slick so that the agency could take commissions on both of their fees. The end result was that he had a lot of time on his hands.

Sometimes Phil and him would go to Blunt but it became more of a hassle as people started to recognise him from the Style Raven ads. Most of the time they just hung out at Phil and Susan's place, drinking and getting stoned while watching the latest movie that Phil had managed to download illegally. Blake preferred going to their place rather than having them at his, because his doorman was on Slick's payroll, and he could never be sure how much of his personal business was relayed to the agency. He regretted moving into a building that was owned by the same company he worked for, but at the time he was just glad to get out of the Broadway. That seemed like such a long time ago.

Blake never knew what sort of mood Susan and Phil would be in when he got there. Initially, she didn't even want him there. Sometimes Blake and Phil did heroin together to come down from all the coke they did. That really pissed off Susan. She complained that the place was turning into a shooting gallery until one night when she needed Blake to give her a shot after she couldn't find a vein and Phil was too drunk to try.

Blake wondered how Phil and Susan had stayed together for so long given that they liked the opposite types of drugs. Susan preferred 'downers,' especially heroin, while Phil liked "up" drugs like coke and meth. When Blake asked Phil what he saw in Susan, he said she would do things that other girls wouldn't do, like "swallow," and that it was easy to keep her under his control because of her habit.

'At least Phil *has* a girlfriend,' Blake lamented to himself. Lots of girls came on to Blake at Blunt, especially the ones that knew he was a model, but he always felt they were judging him or expecting too much. He was usually so stoned by the time they got to his place that he couldn't perform. "Some Style Raven!" one girl laughed the next morning as she walked out the door without even having a coffee. It brought back all the insults he had suffered as a kid.

He'd rather pick up one of the prostitutes from Times Square than a girl at the club. At least he didn't feel like he had to impress them. He liked the older ones, the ones past their sell-by dates, that didn't think he was a freak just for wanting to talk all night. They often came from broken homes like him.

Phil was his only buddy. Everything had happened so fast that he didn't have the time to make friends with other guys. Phil got off on being the friend of the Style Raven model and played it for all it was worth. Unknown to Blake, he got a lot of new customers by offering to introduce them to "the Style Raven guy."

One of the people he introduced to Blake at Blunt was José - the model who hadn't shown up at the photo-session that ended up making Blake a star.

"Hey Blake, this is guy from Slick who you replaced at your first photo-session."

To José, he said, "José, meet your competition, Blake."

Blake wished that Phil hadn't put it that way. He thought José might be upset that he replaced him on the shoot, but he was just excited to meet "the Style Raven guy." Although he knew Blake was straight, he couldn't help thinking he was "hot." He offered to buy him a drink.

"Sure," said Blake, glad that José didn't bare a grudge. "I'll have a whiskey. Actually, why don't I get you a drink? I've got some drink tickets."

José laughed and produced his own wad of drink tickets.

"I see. You can get the next round."

Blake had graduated from screwdrivers to whiskey by then, due to Phil's influence. Phil was a whiskey drinker and always had a bottle at home, so Blake started drinking it too. He turned to ask Phil if he wanted one, but Phil was gone. A customer had dragged him into the men's room.

"I'll get Phil a drink anyway," he said and ordered three whiskies on the rocks from Cameron, then added "but hold the rocks." They laughed.

"Whiskey and air?" Cameron joked, remembering their first conversation.

"Sounds good to me," Blake answered.

"Me too," José said.

Blake asked José how he knew Phil.

"Doesn't everyone?" José responded, pretending to snort a line of coke. He realised he had made a mistake as soon as he saw Blake's face drop. 'José was only eighteen,' Blake thought. 'Phil shouldn't be leading him down the garden path like that.'

On the other hand, Blake wondered if he was any better than Phil. Alcohol was a drug like any other drug and had got José a drink even though he was legally underage. What made that worse than a line of coke? The drinking age in New York was 21 and you were supposed to be 21 to get into the club, but Howie never carded the good-looking guys.

Blake remembered Ava's conversation with Michael at that first photo-session. So, this was José, the guy who had been discovered in the sand dunes! He couldn't help smiling. They stood there, not sure what to say to each other now that Phil wasn't around.

"I hear you're from the Canary Islands. What's it like?" Blake asked.

José was surprised that Blake had heard anything about him.

"Yes, I'm from the Canaries. I lived with my grandmother in the Playa del Ingles area. Have you been there?"

"No, but it sounds nice."

"It is. It's like summertime there all year round."

"Why were you living with your grandmother? Where is the rest of your family?"

"My mother died when I was a kid. She was an addict. She O'D'd. My father has been in prison since I was a kid. He was a gangster, a drug dealer. I don't have contact with him. I only know my grandmother as my mother."

"I'm so sorry to hear that." He felt sorry for José but also envied the close relationship he had with his grandmother. Blake had never even met his own grandmother.

José shrugged. "The Canaries are full of criminals. Most people who live there are hiding away for one reason or another. Even though the islands are officially part of Spain, they have their own laws. They don't have an extradition treaty with America."

Phil had returned by that time, thanked Blake for the drink, and asked if they wanted to do a line. "Sure!" they both said at the same time, and then laughed. Blake's earlier moral reservations quickly disappeared. José couldn't believe he was going to do some coke with the Style Raven guy. Wait until he told his friends in the Canaries. He loved New York. Anything could happen.

After they were finished in the men's room, the three of them went back to the bar. One of the club's photographers took their picture. Phil was off to the side, talking to some of his customers. Once again, he had missed his chance to be in the "What Happened Last Night' section of the club's website. He was only at the bar for a few minutes before he had to leave again to sort more of his customers out.

José was still hyped up on the coke they had done earlier and couldn't stop talking. He told Blake all about the Playa del Ingles and the bars at the Yumbo Centre. There was something for everyone there, apparently - leather bars with backrooms where you could have sex, clubs that stayed open until the next afternoon, a drag bar called Ginger's that had been there since before José was born and was the best place to score coke.

"It sounds great. Are straight people allowed?" Blake asked.

"Of course! The straight bars are closer to the beach, near the boardwalk. But a lot of straights go to Ginger's as well, for the show. You should visit. You could stay at my grandmother's. She would love you. She loves to spoil people. She would treat you like a second son. She's a great cook - traditional Spanish food with fresh ingredients, not like here. Straight from the market. She goes there every morning. Whenever I get paid for a job, I send her some of my money."

He showed Blake a photograph of her on his phone - a tiny grey-haired woman holding onto José for support. "There we are - me and Grandmother Luisa. My friend took it," he explained before kissing the photo and putting the phone back into his pocket.

When Blake and José finished their drinks, Phil appeared out of nowhere - not to pay for the next round but to make sure he was included in it. José insisted on using his drink tickets this time. When Cameron served them, he mentioned that the club would be closing soon. They would have to leave when they finished their drinks. Phil suggested going to the Hole in The Wall after they finished their drinks. Cameron gave him a dirty look.

"The Hole in The Wall?" Blake asked.

Phil shrugged, "What must go up must go down."

"What's the Hole in The Wall?" José asked.

Blake and Phil looked at each other. Blake was willing to go, but he didn't know whether they should drag José into it. Blake asked him if he had ever tried heroin. He hadn't.

"But I'll try anything once!" he said with the exuberance of youth.

"Ok, let's go," Phil said as he downed his drink.

"Hold on Phil, I'm not sure this is a good idea," Blake said, with a glance toward José.

José reassured him: "Don't worry about me, I've done every drug in the world. The Canaries are full of drugs."

Phil ordered a small bottle of water from Cameron: "Don't open it I want to take it with us."

"Hurry up and finish your drinks," Phil said to the others. "I'm not sure how late it stays open."

They quickly finished their drinks and walked downstairs to leave the club. As Cameron wiped down his bar, he thought about Phil. He had heard most of their conversation and he didn't like the influence that Phil had over Blake, or even José, for that matter. José was just a kid. Smack was bad news.

11. The Hole in The Wall

The Hole in The Wall was near Bryant Park, not far from the club. Blake had been there with Phil a few times in the past but had waited for him either in the park or in a nearby alleyway. There was a large dumpster in the alley and sometimes junkies hid behind it while they shot up. The "spotters" - the guys who kept a look-out for the cops - preferred it if people didn't shoot up there - it was too close to where they got the stuff - but there wasn't much they could do about it.

The procedure for scoring was simple. The customer knocked twice on an unmarked door and a peephole opened. Once the pair of eyes looking through the peephole recognised you, two fingers appeared in the hole, took your money and handed over the dope which came in small glassine envelopes like the ones used by stamp collectors. Junkies referred to them as "bags" rather than envelopes. Each "bag" was sealed and stamped with a brand name like "Blackjack," or "Twilight" Some were even named after the U.S. President, or famous fashion labels. It was a form of quality control for the heroin crowd. Different gangs were behind the different "brands" and no gang would dare infringe on another gang's trademark. The strongest brand at the moment was "Liberty."

"It's Liberty!" Phil announced excitedly when he got back to José and Blake who were kneeling behind the dumpster. "I got some syringes too." The spotters also sold disposable syringes for $1.00 each.

"Syringes?" José was surprised. He thought they were going to snort it like cocaine.

Phil told him not to worry, that he could always snort it if he wanted to but shooting it was better.

"Wouldn't he be better to take it back to your place?" Blake asked.

"Nah. Susan will be there. She'll get pissed off if I show up with a stranger. She'll start complaining again about the place becoming a shooting gallery."

Phil went first. He undid his belt and wrapped it around his upper arm to make sure his veins stood out. When he was finished with his shot, he handed the "works" to Blake and leaned against the wall to enjoy his high: "Wow. That's great,"

Blake went next. Phil was right. It was good stuff. He had to stop himself from nodding off while the needle was still in his arm. "Jesus Christ, that's strong," he said to nobody in particular. You could always depend on Liberty.

José couldn't wait for his shot. He couldn't wait to tell his friends in the Canaries that he had done heroin with the Style Raven guy. He pulled up his sleeve like he had seen the others do.

"You do José," Phil said, as he handed the works to Blake and nodded off again.

Blake put more powder in the spoon - "I'm not going to give him a lot because he's never done it before." Phil grunted in agreement, still on the nod.

The belt had fallen on the floor after Blake did his shot and he couldn't find it. Everything was so out of focus. He felt like he was going to black out. "God, that stuff is strong," he repeated.

Phil came to and found the belt. It was under Blake's leg. He helped Blake to tie José off. Blake held the syringe in front of his eyes and tapped it a couple of times to make sure there weren't any air bubbles, then slowly pushed the plunger until a small amount of the liquid could be seen coming out of the needle, just to make sure it was working okay.

"Be careful or you'll waste it," Phil warned. "José, hold out your arm. Wow, great veins. You'll have no problem finding a vein, Blake."

That was the last thing Blake remembered after he woke up from his nod – Phil talking about Jose's veins. When he came to, Phil was standing up beside him, telling him they better go, that it was getting light out. José was still out of it. After his shot, he had nodded off and spread out with his head in Blake's lap.

"We've gotta go Blake, it'll be daylight soon." Phil said. "We don't want to be here when they come to empty the trash."

Blake shook José to wake him up. "José, c'mon we've got to get out of here," he mumbled.

There was no response.

Phil gave José a gentle kick: "José, get up. We've gotta go."

Nothing.

"Thank god I only put a small amount in the spoon," Blake said, shaking him again. "José, it's time to go."

Still nothing.

Phil knelt down. "José, are you okay?"

No answer.

Phil tried to find a pulse, first in José's wrists and then in his neck. Nothing. He looked at Blake. "I can't find a pulse."

Blake shook José again. He was starting to panic: "GET UP, José!"

José didn't move. Blake looked at Phil, terrified.

"He's not going to get up," Phil said. "He doesn't have a pulse. He's dead, Blake. José is dead."

"But I gave him such a small amount."

"Did you use the same cotton?"

"Well, yeah, I mean it was in the spoon..."

"Blake, it was his first time. There was probably enough left in the cotton to get him high. And then you added more. It was strong stuff."

Blake didn't know what to say. Everything seemed so unreal. Phil took control, as if he had gone into automatic pilot. He didn't mention it, but he had been through this before. Not with Blake, but with a friend of Susan's - an ex-friend. He knew they had to work fast before rigor mortis set in.

"Blake, we've got to get rid of the body. You've got to help me get it into the dumpster. We have to get out of here. Quick,"

"But we killed him. We need to call the police."

"No, Blake, *you* killed him. You were the one who gave him the shot. You pulled the trigger. Now snap out of it and help me with his body."

"But..."

"Shut up, Blake. We've got to get rid of the body. He won't be the first junkie to die of an overdose in New York."

Phil lifted José by his shoulders and told Blake to take his legs.

"Thank god, you're so tall" he said, as they tried to get the body into the dumpster which was taller than both of them. They finally got it over the side; they could hear the body fall onto the trash that was already in there. The whole process took minutes, maybe not even a minute, but it felt like forever.

"C'mon, let's get out of here," Phil said.

They were so eager to leave the scene of their crime that they didn't notice the spotter standing at the other end of the alleyway who had seen just about everything.

"Walk fast," Phil instructed Blake calmly, "but not too fast. We're just two guys walking home after a night out. Nobody has to know a thing…"

"He was so young…" Blake interrupted, dazed.

"Get a grip, you idiot. It happens all the time."

Blake stopped walking. "But his grandmother, what about his grandmother?" he asked, remembering the picture that José had shown him, and how he had said he could stay with them if he ever went to the Canaries. Who was going to tell the grandmother?

"Don't worry about it," Phil continued: "And listen, it would be best if we didn't see each other for a while. Don't say anything to anyone about what happened. If you need some stuff, go to the Hole in The Wall and tell them you're a friend of Phil the Goon. That's what they call me. I'll give them your name, not your real name – you've got to have a nickname. I'll tell them that you're called Black and Blue because of your black hair and blue eyes."

"Phil, I've got to go to the police. I've just killed someone."

Phil grabbed him by the shoulders. "Don't say anything to anyone! Do you understand? Stop panicking! Do you know how many overdoses there are every night in this city? If someone mentions it, don't say anything. José was your competition. How would that look? There's nothing you can do about it now, anyway. It's finished. Over. Just go on living like you used to. Don't let it ruin your success. You can't change the past."

Success? Was that all that Phil cared about? Success at what cost? Blake remembered he had a photo-session tomorrow. How could he get through it, after what he'd been through? He didn't give a shit about success.

When they arrived outside Blake's building, Phil said "You're home now Blake. Forget about it. And for god's sake, don't talk to the police. Don't panic. Everything is going to be alright. I'm going home. If you see me at Blunt, ignore me."

Blunt was the last thing on Blake's mind. How could Phil want to go to Blunt anymore? He let himself into the lobby of his building, passing the doorman at the front desk who nodded as he passed. The doorman was used to tenants coming home late, especially Blake. He watched him get into the elevator and then went outside to have a cigarette. He hardly noticed the back of a man who was hurrying away from the building on his way home.

12. Disco!

"Get ready to Disco!"

Blake stood in a pair of Moschino bellbottoms decorated with Andy Warhol's *Flowers* while Chic played in the background. The photographer was telling everyone to "Dance, dance, dance," and moved amongst them with a handheld camera to get shots of them dancing. He wanted it to seem as amateurish as possible - like someone had taken the shots with an old disposable camera.

Blake didn't feel like dancing. He felt tired and grumpy and worried. He couldn't get José's death out of his mind. As stoned as he was last night, he couldn't sleep and when he did, he had nightmares. Instead of the "success" Phil had told him to concentrate on, he kept on hearing his father's voice calling him a failure. He woke up screaming several times. In one dream, he watched José's head fall into his lap and crack like broken glass.

"Blake!" the photographer shouted. "Get with it, man. Don't worry if you can't dance – I'm not shooting a movie. Just pose in weird positions. And smile like you're having fun. You look absolutely miserable."

After the Chic song ended, Odyssey's "Native New Yorker" began. Blake did his best. He moved his body into different positions as the lyrics of the song went through his head: "you should know the score by now, you're a native New Yorker...."

When the song was over, the photographer's assistant played it again. Over and over and over. "I love this song," he said, as he continued to sing along, "Where did all those yesterdays go? When you still believed life could really be like a Broadway show. You were the star, when did it close?..."

At the end of the shoot, the photographer asked Blake what was wrong. He shrugged, got dressed and walked out the studio door.

"See you tomorrow!" the photographer yelled after him. They were supposed to finish the photo-session tomorrow.

As the door shut, Blake heard the photographer's assistant say, "Get *her*!"

Blake didn't know whether he could work another day. He couldn't get José and his grandmother out of his head. On the way home he passed a police station and wondered if he should go in and confess. That would be the 'right' thing to do. But what good would it do? It wouldn't bring José back. And it could get Phil into trouble. He knew Phil wasn't perfect, but he had been Blake's only friend. He wished he could call him, even after what they had been through – or maybe because of it.

At home Blake turned on the news but there was no mention of the murder. He checked the internet; no mention there either. He felt a mixture of relief and remorse. There were so many grisly murders in New York that nobody cared about poor José.

He laid down on the couch and tried to stop thinking. Usually, he'd be getting ready to go out by this time. He wondered what Phil was doing. He was probably sitting at home nodding off happily with Susan, having already scored for her. He remembered what Phil had said - that he was going to tell the guy at the Hole in The Wall that Blake's nickname was "Black and Blue." He thought about going to score, but it would be like returning to the scene of the crime. What if there were police in the alley?

He could use a hit. But was it worth the risk? At least he would be able to sleep. He didn't want to show up for the shoot tomorrow looking like he hadn't had any sleep, again. Gossip spread so quickly in the fashion industry. Did he really care? How could he even think of scoring after what had happened to José?

'To score or not to score' was the question, and it was driving him crazy. He got an empty coffee cup from the kitchen cupboard and set it on the glass coffee table in front of the couch. He rolled up a piece of paper into a ball and he decided that if he made 'a basket' - managed to throw the ball into the cup - that he would get some dope. If he missed, he would stay at home. He threw the ball; it hit the edge of the cup and fell on the floor. Decision made. He had missed. He would stay home.

Fifteen minutes later he was on his way to the Hole in The Wall.

* * * * *

Blake had to walk past the alley to score. The dumpster was gone but there was no 'crime scene' tape or any other indication that an incident had taken place. Maybe Phil was right. If they just kept their mouths shut, the police would just consider José's death as one of many overdoses that occurred nightly in New York. He wondered if Phil had told Susan about what happened.

Blake went to the appropriate door and knocked two times.

A voice asked who it was. He answered "Black and Blue" feeling like an idiot. A small hatch opened, he handed over $20, and was given a glassine envelope. As he put it into his pocket, he noticed it wasn't "Liberty," it was "Green Tape." He'd had it before. It wasn't as strong as "Liberty" but at least he hadn't been ripped off. His mood lightened. Scoring by himself made him feel like he belonged to a secret club. He was looking forward to getting stoned.

When he got home, he dipped his finger into the powder he had just bought and snorted a small amount. A familiar warmth spread throughout his body. He wished he had got a syringe but was glad that he hadn't. This was a one-off. The last thing he wanted was to develop a habit. He nodded off and started dreaming. This time the dreams weren't so bad. He was at a carnival and everyone was happy and eating cotton candy and a woman was singing sweetly in the background; his mother.

The next thing he knew the alarm on his phone was going off and he had to rush to the photo-session. He was in a better mood this time. He was still high when he arrived at the studio, and he snorted more from the bag during the break for lunch. He made a mental note to get a pack of syringes on his way home after the shoot. He'd stop by the pharmacy that Phil had told him about. There was only a small amount of dope left after lunch and he knew that he would get higher from shooting it.

He was exhausted by the end of the day. As soon as he got back to his apartment, he had a hit and felt better, although there wasn't as much dope left as he thought. He went back to the Hole in The Wall. This time he bought five bags. He figured that it would get him through the rest of the week, maybe longer if he injected each time. He could quit at the end of the week. A week's worth of dope wasn't going to give him withdrawals, at least not bad ones.

On the way to score, he passed the alley again and there was nothing there - no dumpster and, more importantly, still no indication that it was a crime scene. They had probably moved the dumpster someplace else. Too many junkies shot up behind it. Moving it probably had nothing to do with José. He wished he hadn't thought of José. He wondered if his grandmother knew yet. What would she do without her grandson?

Back at home, Blake did half a bag with the needle he used before. He had lucked out - it was "Liberty" this time. He felt the effect of the shot, instantly. Scratching his nose, he flushed the needle out and left it in a glass, to be used again tomorrow. It was a disposable, and should have only been used once, but that doesn't matter to an addict. Addicts used disposable syringes until the point becomes too dull to force into a vein.

After nodding off for about half an hour - or was it an hour or two - Blake got on his computer and looked for any news about José's murder. Still nothing. Phil was right. Everything was going to be okay.

13. Lieutenant Warren

Lieutenant Harry Warren sat at his desk, looking out the window, bored shitless. 'I thought New York was supposed to be the crime capital of the world,' he mumbled to himself as he went through the inbox on his computer. The only cases he seemed to get nowadays were ones that involved a lot of forms. Desk cases they called them because you didn't have to leave your desk to deal with them. Compared to what he had dealt with before his cardiac arrest, they were kid's stuff. He had joined the force to hunt down criminals on foot, gun drawn, like he had seen on old movies on TV, not to sit at a desk all day filling out forms on his computer and looking out the window at the bums hustling tourists.

Maybe his boss, Captain Seligman, was right when he suggested an early retirement for medical reasons. But to a young cop like Warren, an early retirement was like a living death. He had been the force's golden boy at one time – the cop who put Dr. John Gilman into prison for life. The Gilman case had been every cop's dream and nightmare - a serial murderer posing as a psychiatrist who got inside women's apartments by getting inside their minds. Rich woman who could afford a psychiatrist - society types or women who worked in the fashion business. Not models but the women in power who ran the agencies. The public lapped it up because it gave them an insider's view of a world that they had only read about in the gossip pages. The press had a field day with the case, with headlines about "The Patient Murderer," which, as time went by, became "NYPD Fails Again to Stop the Patient Murderer." That's when Warren was brought in.

A lot of the evidence against Gilman had already been collected by that time, but it was Warren who made the final arrest which turned him into a national hero. The psycho psychiatrist had left his DNA in his last victim's penthouse, but it was Warren who came up with the idea of getting an undercover colleague, Angela Williams, to pose as a socialite newly arrived from the west coast. She made an appointment for a home visit with the psychiatrist who was more than happy to oblige. "Home" was a large suite in the St. Regis.

First, Gilman hypnotised her (or thought he did); then he proceeded to strangle her with his belt. Warren popped out of a closet, gun drawn, and made the arrest. The underside of the belt had a raised designer emblem on it; its imprint had been noticed on the neck of some of his other victims.

After his arrest, Gilman confessed to even more murders than he was being investigated for. He wasn't a medical doctor at all. He had a PhD in philosophy, not psychology, and a hatred of rich women that stemmed from his mother who had left her kid mostly with the staff as she drank her way through the high life until she became his first victim. After getting a taste for murder, he couldn't stop until Warren stepped in.

The press loved Harry Warren. With his thick brown hair and bulging biceps, he looked like a cop you'd see in the movies. He even did a fashion shoot for *Gentleman's Monthly* after he was promoted from Senior Investigator to Lieutenant. He loved being a hero so much that he tried to become one again with disastrous results. A year after his promotion, he stupidly chased a known drug dealer down the middle of the street after seeing him push a little old lady into oncoming traffic on 5th Avenue. He heard the woman scream and ran to help. It was a natural reaction for a cop, even an off-duty one. But the traffic on 5th Avenue didn't stop. He got hit by a driver who was never found. While he was lying in the street, waiting for the ambulance, he had a heart attack which turned into a cardiac arrest in the ambulance. He had a few broken bones, but it was the cardiac arrest that kept him in the hospital for two months. They never found the driver who hit him. The 'old lady' he tried to save turned out to be a dealer who was encroaching on the other dealer's turf. His career had been ruined by trying to protect one dealer from another.

When Warren got out of the hospital, Captain Seligman suggested that he resign for medical reasons. He would get a good severance package and could keep his pension. He refused. He felt that he was still young – in his late thirties - and still had a lot to give to the force. If he was going to leave, he wanted to leave on a high, not after a failure like that stupid "accident."

The union backed up Warren, but they couldn't stop Seligman from relegating him to the position of digital paper pusher. Seligman argued that it was too risky to give a cop with heart disease a major assignment. What if he had another heart attack?

Warren didn't bear Seligman a grudge. They had known each other too long for that. He could understand his boss's reticence at giving him a major case, but that didn't stop him from wanting one. The force made what use of him they could. When they needed a good-looking cop to talk to the press about a case, they used him as a spokesman. The media still loved him. His heart disease hadn't affected his movie-star looks. He felt that if he could just hang on a little longer, a case would come his way that would restore his reputation and then, maybe, just maybe, he would be willing to take an early retirement. Or maybe he wouldn't need to anymore. Just one more important case. That's all he needed.

So, he was surprised and a little bit excited to see, as he was going through his inbox on that "bored shitless" morning, an email from his boss with "Fernandez, José - Potential Murder" on the subject line.

Murder? Things were looking up. He opened the file and saw a photograph of an attractive 18-year-old that looked like a headshot from a model's portfolio. Maybe the guy was famous. As he read through the details of the case, however, his enthusiasm waned considerably. This wasn't a murder; it was an overdose. Even worse, it was probably accidental. He rang his boss.

"Why have I got this email about Fernandez?" Warren asked. "Shouldn't it go to Narcotics?"

"Probably. But I'm giving it to you."

"So that we can say we did something about it without doing anything about it?"

"I hope that's not a criticism of the fine work of the force."

"Of course not."

"Good. Could you come to my office so we can discuss the case?"

"Sure."

When Warren got to his boss' office, Seligman explained, "Narcotics already knows about the case but they're so busy with the mobsters who are taking over this city, they asked if I could get someone from our department to look into it. Fernandez' grandmother has been calling them every day from the Canary Islands and she's threatening to make a big thing about her grandson's death in the local newspaper. That's all we need - bad press in Spain that will be picked up by the New York media in a matter of nano seconds."

Harry laughed. "Ok, ok, I'll look into it for Grandma then. Where was the body found?"

"What body?"

"You don't have a body?"

"Well, not exactly. A finger maybe."

"Huh? What happened to the body that was attached to the finger?"

"It sort of got mashed up."

"What do you mean mashed up? Do you mean like mash potatoes?"

"Yeah. That's it. Like mash potatoes. It was in a dumpster and all the trash in the dumpster went through a mashing machine."

"What the fuck is a mashing machine?"

"It mashes up trash for transport abroad. You'd be surprised how much New York trash ends up in Thailand."

"I met some of that trash when I worked in Vice."

"That's not the type of trash I'm talking about. Anyway, as I was saying before I was interrupted, one of the guys who operates the mashing machine lives with a dog."

"A real one?"

"Yes, a real one. He brings it into work sometimes. On this particular day, the dog found a finger in the trash that didn't get mashed up. He took it to his owner in his mouth. That's how they identified the model."

"I think I'm going to be sick. It says in the file that the guy who overdosed was signed to the Slick Agency. I'm familiar with the agency - you know I am because of the Gilman case. One of his victims was the head of Hair and Make-up there."

"Exactly. That's why I thought you would be good for the case. You already have a connection."

"No, you thought I'd be good for the case because it would give me something to do."

"Warren, there was enough heroin in that finger to kill most people - not most addicts - but most people. So, who knows? Maybe it was accidental and maybe it wasn't. All I know is that there's a persistent grandmother in the Canaries, who probably watches too many late-night detective shows, who thinks her grandson was bumped off by evil New York gangsters. She's never even been to New York. All we have to do is to convince her it was an accidental overdose. Nobody was trying to kill her grandson."

"I see. So, I was right. It is another token case. Any chance of getting something meatier in the future – no pun intended?"

"Harry, I'd love to get you back on the streets, but I'd never forgive myself if you had another heart attack. And how would it look in the press? The offer about early retirement still stands. I'll make it worth your while. Take advantage of it while you can."

"No thanks. Anything else I need to know about this case?"

"Just what's in the file. The last photo we have of Fernandez is him and the Style Raven guy in the V.I.P room at Blunt."

"Style Raven?"

"Yeah, the model they use on the Style Raven products - men's grooming stuff like hair gel and shaving cream - that sort of thing. His name is Blake Webster. I wouldn't make too much of it. It could have been a coincidence that they were at the bar at the same time, but it's probably worth a visit to Webster. I rang his agency and spoke to the woman who runs the men's division – Ava."

"I know Ava."

"She told me Blake is at a photo-session today and gave me the details."

The case was beginning to sound more interesting. Style Raven was a famous brand. There was bound to be press interest if the Style Raven guy was involved. If a V.I.P. room was also involved, even better. Maybe it would turn out to be a bigger case than Seligman thought it was. Maybe it was the case that Warren had been waiting for. He took down the details of the photo-session but there were two people he wanted to visit first: Ava and Luigi.

14. Ava and Luigi

Lieutenant Warren hoped that that Ava and Luigi would be able to fill him in on any personal information about Blake that hadn't made it into the case file and might come in handy when he interviewed him later that afternoon. He had already checked to see if Blake had a criminal record of any type or had incriminated himself on social media but hadn't come up with anything. How could anyone be *that* innocent? Webster seemed largely absent from life until he suddenly became the face of Style Raven.

Ava was talking to her secretary in her outer office when Warren knocked lightly on the door and let himself in.

"Harry! What a wonderful surprise!" she said. "Please, come into my office."

As they walked into her office, the wheels in her brain had already started turning. 'What did he want?' she wondered. She hoped that one of her models wasn't in trouble. Or that she wasn't.

Warren sat down at her desk. "I'm sorry to have to tell you this but one of your models has died."

"What! Who?"

"José Fernandez. He works for you, doesn't he?"

"Oh my god," she gasped. "Poor darling José. What on earth happened?" She was sorry to hear about José, but couldn't help feeling relieved that nothing had happened to one of her high earners.

"Overdose. Maybe accidental. Maybe murder."

"Oh. I don't know what to say. He was so young. A new signing. I didn't really know him. One of our photographers or stylists or somebody discovered him while they were on vacation in the Canary Islands. He was working as a waiter at a place called the Yumbo Centre." She left out the part about the dunes.

"Did he do drugs?"

"Who knows?" She looked down at her top drawer to make sure it was closed. "I try not to get involved in the personal lives of my models. I almost fired him when he didn't show up for his first photo-session, but you know me, I'm a softy, especially when it comes to the young ones. Sometimes I feel more like a mother than a boss."

'More like an evil stepmother,' Warren thought. He showed her the picture of José and Blake at the bar. "This is the last picture we have of him. At Blunt with one of your other models - Blake Webster. Were they close friends?"

Ava laughed. "If you mean, were they lovers, you are certainly barking up the wrong tree with that one! Blake is straight. It wasn't a lover's spat, if that's what you're getting at. Blake used to be a farmer in California - or something like that. It's in his bio."

Warren got the impression that Ava saw Jose's death as nothing more than the loss of a commodity – a product she wouldn't be able to sell anymore. Models weren't human beings, they were "bios."

"What do you think they were doing at the bar together?" he asked her.

"Having a drink?" Ava suggested with more than a hint of sarcasm. "It's not unusual for two models from the same agency to have a drink together in the V.I.P. room at Blunt."

"How did you know it was the V.I.P. room?"

"Isn't that Cameron serving them? Everyone knows Cameron."

"Ava, we go back a long way. You really helped me out with the Gilman case. I'm going to ask you something and I want a truthful answer. Does Blake do drugs?"

"Drugs! I doubt it. Blake's a small-town boy. I'm surprised to see him at the bar in that picture. I practically had to beg him to have a glass of champagne when I signed him. I don't even think he knew what champagne was. He certainly couldn't use chopsticks, that was for sure."

Warren couldn't use chopsticks either, but that was beside the point. He put the photograph in his briefcase, feeling slightly dejected. Maybe this wasn't going to be the big case he was hoping for, after all.

"I can vouch for Blake. He doesn't do drugs. And he certainly doesn't do murder."

"Thanks anyway, Ava. I appreciate your time. If you find out anything, can you let me know?" He handed her his card as he started to leave.

"I most certainly will," she said as she took the card. "Warren, one other thing that I'm sure that you, more than anyone, are aware of - an overdose isn't a particularly rare event in this city. I mean, José wasn't even famous..."

"No Ava, he wasn't even famous," he repeated as he walked out the office door wondering what was wrong with the world.

* * * * *

The next stop was Gigi's. Luigi kept up with New York's fashion gossip through the Slick models who used his diner for their caffeine fixes on their breaks. During the Gilman case, the psychiatrist's name had popped up a lot in their conversations, which he had relayed to Lieutenant Warren. Although the force rightly suspected that Luigi had something to do with the cocaine that was flooding the New York clubs, they turned the other cheek because, for the moment at least, he was more helpful as a source of information than as a suspect; they wanted to keep him on their side.

Luigi greeted the Lieutenant with open arms, like they were old friends, He treated most cops like that. And most criminals.

"Let's go into the office," he said to Warren who followed him into the storeroom. They sat at Luigi's desk, surrounded by boxes of Panettone that contained enough cocaine to supply the entire New York club scene for more than a month.

"What's up?" Luigi asked Warren from his side of the desk.

Warren showed him the picture of José and Blake at Blunt: "Can you tell me anything about them?"

Luigi was as surprised as Ava to see that Blake was in the picture.

"José stops in here now and then, not much. He's new to Slick. Blake has been around awhile. A nice guy. He's the Style Raven guy. Why?"

"We're trying to find out more about José. This is the last picture we have of him. He died of an overdose."

"I'm sorry to hear that. What does it have to do with Blake?"

"I'm not sure. Is Blake a drug user?"

Luigi basically said the same thing as Ava: "Are you joking? He's a small-town guy. I doubt it." Then he noticed something about the photo. He held it up for a closer look, and then returned it to the desk.

"No, Blake's as clean as they come," he said. "I think you've hit a dead end there. They were probably just having a drink together. Have you been to Slick?"

"Yeah, I talked to Ava. But she basically said the same thing - that Blake hardly drank, let alone did drugs."

"What did José overdose from?"

"Heroin."

"Heroin?"

"He overdosed from heroin."

"Where did he get it?"

"That's one of the things I'm trying to find out."

"Sorry, but I can't be of much help on this one. I wish I could. If I hear anything I'll let you know." He stood up to show the lieutenant out of the office. "And, please, Warren, don't be such a stranger. Anytime you want a coffee, it's on the house."

"Thanks, I may take you up on that."

"You're always welcome," Luigi lied.

As soon as Warren was out the door, Luigi got on the phone to Phil. The reason he had looked closer at the photograph was that he noticed a detail that both Warren and his boss had ignored – a partial image of somebody's hand on the bar next to José and Blake. They must have thought it was another customer waiting to be served but there was a ring on one of the fingers. You could only see part of it, but Luigi recognised it as Phil's ring - a gold signet ring with the letter C embossed on it. It was a gift from Susan on his last birthday. He remembered when Phil first showed it to him.

"What a piece of shit," Luigi had said at the time. "It's gold-plated and do you really want to walk around with a "C" on your finger, broadcasting to the world that you're a coke dealer? *Stupido!*"

Phil usually left it at home after that but sometimes he wore it out at night and the night of the photograph was one of those times. When he finally answered his uncle's phone call, Luigi screamed into the phone: "What the fuck are you up to?"

"Well, for one thing I was trying to get some sleep," Phil answered. Late night last night."

"Let me guess. Blunt again?"

"No, actually I went to Arena. I've been staying away from Blunt."

"And why might that be?"

"No particular reason. Just got a bit bored. I do go to other clubs you know."

"What the fuck do you have to do with this dead model?"

It was impossible not to notice the silent pause before Phil answered, "What dead model?"

"Some guy called José. That lieutenant was just here.

Warren. The one from the Gilman case."

"What did he say?"

"He was asking about Blake."

"Why?"

"Because he has a photo of the two of them at the bar at Blunt and your hand is in it with that goddamn piece of shit ring from that goddamn piece of shit junkie girlfriend of yours. Thank god you could only see part of the 'C' in the photo."

"Don't worry. I didn't have anything to do with a dead model. I was just waiting for a drink. Even if they recognise the ring, I was just waiting for a drink. I don't always wear it. I happened to be wearing it that night."

What happened that night?"

"How should I know?"

"I shouldn't have asked. I'm not involved. But Phil, can you do me a favour?"

"Sure, Uncle Luigi."

"How many times do I have to tell you not to call me uncle!" he shouted.

"Ok, ok."

"Get rid of that fake piece of shit of a ring. I don't care what you do with it - flush it down the toilet or throw it in the river but get rid of it. It could become evidence."

"But I didn't do anything."

"Sure, you didn't, you idiot. Just don't get me involved. I don't want to know anything."

"How could you be involved when I'm not involved?"

"Don't be so smart. What time are you coming over for dinner on Sunday?"

"I don't know. I guess lunchtime. 2:00?"

"Don't bring your girlfriend. She's nothing but trouble, with that habit of hers. The last time she was at the house, she nodded off in her spaghetti."

"She's better now. She signed up to that methadone clinic near the Broadway."

It was true. After Phil told Susan about what happened to José, she registered with the methadone maintenance program that operated out of the church near Blake's hotel. During the first few weeks she had to attend the clinic daily and swallow her dose in front of a nurse, to make sure she wasn't squirrelling it away in her cheek to sell outside the clinic. Some patients were actually caught doing that. They would transfer their dose to a buyer's mouth after they left the clinic.

Patients were given random blood tests. If they didn't test positive for other drugs after the first three weeks, they only had to go to the clinic twice a week. They'd be given take home doses in small plastic bottles for the days they weren't at the clinic. They could even request two weeks' worth of the drug if they had an emergency or were going on holiday, providing they passed their blood tests.

"So now she's getting high on the taxpayer's money. Is that it?" Luigi asked. "For how hard I work every day, a seventy-year-old man, and she's getting high for free off my taxes?"

"Don't worry I won't bring her." Phil said.

His uncle had a point. Susan was higher now than she had ever been on heroin. Anytime she felt the urge to score, she told her counsellor at the clinic, and they upped her dose of methadone. She had started at 40 mg. per day; by the end of the month, she had graduated to 90 mg.

Like most of the patients, Susan didn't drink all of her take-home doses. She saved a small amount from each bottle for her "emergency supply" which she kept in an empty bottle in the fridge. She still got high as a kite from the amount that was left. She could sit and do nothing for hours. Phil called her his "little zombie." She thought it was cute.

* * * * *

Warren, meanwhile, was on his way to the studio where Blake was doing his photo-session. He hadn't told Ava or Luigi that he was going to see Blake because he didn't want them to warn him. He wanted to see how he reacted when a cop appeared out of nowhere; if he broke out in a sweat or seemed nervous, it might be an indication of guilt.

There wasn't an elevator in the four-floor walk-up where the studio was located, so the lieutenant had to take the stairs. By the time he got to the top floor, he was having chest pains - if his boss needed proof that he should retire for medical reasons, this was it. But he never mentioned his chest pains to Seligman - it would just give him an excuse to force him into an early retirement which, as a young cop, he saw as a living death. He reached for the GT spray he kept in his jacket pocket and sprayed it under his tongue twice. He hated the stuff. It gave him a headache - like inhaling turpentine - but it opened up his arteries and relieved the pain.

Someone must have heard him in the hallway because the studio door creaked open slightly and Warren saw a pair of eyelashes looking at him - one of the models. He showed his NYPD identification card and she let him in.

"Who is it?" the photographer shouted. He was shooting Blake on a fake bull in front of a green screen.

"A cop," the model answered as she popped a bubble from the gum she was chewing.

"Ditch the gum, Jennifer, it's fucking up your lipstick," the photographer warned.

Warren looked at Blake and tried to figure out if the worried expression on his face was an indication of guilt. The problem was that everyone in the room looked guilty. Most of them were trying to remember if they had left any illegal substances in their street clothes that were hanging on a rail near the studio entrance. Thank god the cop hadn't brought any dogs.

Warren asked the photographer if he could borrow Blake for a few minutes.

"Sure, go ahead," he said. "This shoot is costing us hundreds of dollars a minute, so don't mind me. I'm just the photographer!"

"Thanks. I'm sure the force appreciates you fulfilling your civic duty."

As Blake got off the bull and went to the back of the studio with Warren, the photographer mumbled "civic duty my ass," to his assistant.

"They look like the beginning of a gay porn film," the assistant commented, as he watched the cop with the movie-star looks and blue-eyed Blake retreat to a corner of the studio.

Blake tried to stay calm, but there was so much to be nervous about. He wasn't just thinking about José, he was also worried that the lieutenant would notice his pinned pupils. The first thing that Warren did was to take out the photograph of José and Blake at Blunt. 'Do you remember that night?' he asked.

"Yeah, of course I do. We had a short conversation, nothing special. Model talk. Our last jobs, that sort of thing."

."What did he say was his last job?"

Blake didn't know what to say because they hadn't talked about that at all.

"I can't remember. The night was sort of a blur. Too many whiskies."

Warren laughed. "I know that feeling."

Although Blake's answer wasn't very satisfying, his demeanour was. Warren felt that he had become a pretty good judge of character during his years in the force and Blake wasn't acting like a guilty person. He remained calm when he saw the photo and answered the few questions that the lieutenant asked with a politeness that made Warren agree with Ava and Luigi. He was a likeable, refreshingly honest young man with a small-town mentality. If he hadn't become a model, he would probably have made a good cop. When Warren got back to his office, he reported to Seligman that there probably wasn't a case. Blake was innocent.

"Did you ask him how José could have got into that dumpster on his own?" Seligman asked.

"Well, no, but he said that they just had a short conversation at the bar. I believed him."

"Did you ask him where he went after the club closed, or who he was with?"

"There didn't seem to be any reason to. I'm sure he was telling the truth. I also visited Ava and Luigi and they didn't think that Blake was doing drugs either. Both of them vouched for him."

"I wouldn't trust that Italian's opinion on anything," Seligman responded, referring to Luigi.

"Well, I'm a pretty good judge of character and Blake seemed like a nice guy."

"Don't worry about it, I was just playing devil's advocate," Seligman said. "While you were out, a Spanish newspaper called and asked about the case. The reporter said they was being hassled by the grandmother who seemed to think New York was full of gangsters just waiting to get hold of her 'famous' grandson. I told him there wasn't a case. It was just another accidental overdose. Case closed."

"Case closed," Warren repeated. He was almost disappointed that it was just another overdose. Neither of them thought to interview Cameron, the bartender that Ava mentioned, or the person whose hand was in the photograph that Luigi had noticed.

15. The Downfall

Blake had managed to keep his cool in front of Lieutenant Warren but as soon as the lieutenant left, he did what Phil had warned him not to do. He panicked. They continued with the shoot, but he couldn't concentrate. He had to try too hard to be "natural."

"Blake, what is wrong with you?" the photographer asked.

"I'm not feeling well."

"Fuck it, Blake. Let's just go home."

As they were changing into their street clothes one of the other models asked Blake what was wrong.

"Nothing."

"What did that cop say?"

"Nothing."

It didn't take long for the word to spread that a cop had been at the shoot and had questioned Blake.

On his way home, Blake passed the same police station he had passed before and again considered turning himself in. How much longer could he live with this level of anxiety? He wondered what the sentence was for manslaughter. After all, he hadn't intended to kill José. It was all a horrible accident. But how could he prove it? Phil was right when he said José was his competition. Was that what Phil would say if it ever went to court? Plea-bargain his way to freedom by testifying that Blake had murdered his competition on purpose? He was glad the photo-session ended early. There was dope waiting at home; at least he had *that* to look forward to.

It wasn't long before Blake was sitting on his couch in his living room, sticking a needle into his arm and feeling his problems disappear. If there was a pill that people could take to get rid of their problems, wouldn't they? The only difference was that he was using a needle. But he liked the needle. He liked the preparation that went with the drug. It had become a familiar ritual that, in itself, provided him with comfort.

He drew the plunger back three times, just to make sure he got every little bit. Then he flushed the syringe with water and put his works into the kitchen drawer where he had been keeping his dope. He reached his hand to the back of the drawer and pulled out a small glassine bag that was still sealed - tomorrow's dose. It was the only one left. He was surprised – had he really gone through a week's supply in a few days? He had lost track of how much he was doing. He was glad it was his last bag. He would quit after that.

He had a peaceful sleep that night. When he woke the next morning, he decided to treat himself to a small hit so he wouldn't be in a bad mood at work. He had planned to leave the bag alone until he got back from the shoot, but he figured a small hit wouldn't hurt. The last thing he wanted was to be clucking at work.

He did the rest of the bag when he got home. It wasn't enough. He ended up at the Hole in The Wall again. He only got one bag because he was going to quit tomorrow, but when tomorrow came, he needed another bag. So, he scored again, and again and again. When he used up the veins in his arms, he shot up in the back of his hand. The dark circles under his eyes became deeper and his weight loss more pronounced. His blue eyes became bluer because his pupils were so pinned. It looked good at first, but his eyes were too sunken, his body too gaunt. Photographers began to complain. He didn't look like the boy next door anymore, he looked like the junkie next door.

It wasn't long before Ava called him into the office. Since her conversation with Warren, she had kept an eye on Blake - not her eye but the eyes of the network of bookers, assistants and photographers who worked for her. They were happy to dish the dirt, even old dirt about hanging out with Phil at Blunt. Some photographers complained directly to her about Blake showing up late at shoots or not showing up at all. And when he did show up, he couldn't wait to get home. He was "weird."

Ava had to take action. He was giving the agency a bad name. She had been through it with other models, but she never expected it to happen to Blake. His addiction was out of control. She called him into her office. When he arrived, her secretary buzzed the intercom and told her "Mr. Webster" was here. Ava told her to ask him to wait. He sat down and waited. He knew something was up because he was no longer getting the V.I.P. treatment.

While Blake waited in the outer office, Ava opened her top drawer and quickly snorted a line of coke. Her three prepared lines had doubled - now there were six lines that she allowed herself throughout the day. Sometimes, on long days, she would do half a line at a time, making her allocation last even longer. It was all under control. That was the important thing. To keep it under control. She could trust herself, but she couldn't trust Blake. After the line she had just snorted worked its way down the back of her throat, she pushed a button on her desk and told her secretary that she would see "Mr. Webster" now.

She was standing behind her desk when he walked in. There were no "hello" kisses. It was like he had a disease. She was shocked at how thin he had become.

"Blake, darling, thank you for coming, please sit down," she said from her side of the desk.

He sat down. He wondered if the police had visited her about José. Did she know something that he didn't? Had they told her he was a suspect? Maybe she didn't want to get near him because she was afraid of him. Maybe she thought that he would hurt her too. He wished he had the nerve. He felt betrayed by the people he had met in New York and wouldn't mind wringing a few of their necks.

"Blake, look, I'll cut to the point. I don't care what models do when they're not modelling - that's up to them. I don't pry..." she said, almost believing it.

Blake could tell what was coming. She was kicking him out of the agency.

"But I've been getting complaints from some important people. You didn't show up on a couple of jobs and when you do show up, you're a mess. That's how one person described it - a 'mess.'"

"I've always called at least a day in advance if I was too ill to show up."

"Blake, *look at you*! What happened to that innocent farm boy I hired a year ago? *What happened Blake?*"

He didn't say anything. What could he say? Murder. That's what happened. He had killed a young man whose grandmother would never be able to see him again. Is that what she wanted him to say?

"I'm really sorry Blake, I really am," she continued in a voice dripping with fake sincerity. "I'm going to have to let you go."

He should have been upset but he didn't care anymore. Being fired was a relief. It meant he could go home and have a hit. He hated modelling and all the phoniness that went with it.

Ava continued. "It's not all bad news, Blake. The Style Raven contract continues until the end of the year, so you'll still get your royalty payments until then, plus bits and pieces that

Slick still owes you. I'm sure you'll have no trouble getting work with other agencies. You can depend on me for a recommendation if you need one."

She walked to his side of the desk and stretched out her arms: "Oh Blake!" He stood up and received her hug, his arms hanging loosely by his sides.

"Still friends?" she asked cheerfully.

"Sure."

She went back to her seat: "Oh good. I would hate to leave on bad terms."

He stayed standing. Then the bomb dropped.

"Oh, I almost forgot," she said. "This means, of course, that you'll have to move from the apartment. But don't worry, we'll give you until the end of the month to find someplace else. With your Style Raven money coming in, I'm sure you'll have no problem finding a new apartment."

He was shocked. It was like she had stabbed him in the back and was now turning the knife. He forgot that the agency owned the apartment. He could accept being jobless but not homeless. It was a hassle to look for a place in New York. The monthly payment he got from Style Raven just wasn't enough to pay for both an apartment and a heroin habit.

"Make sure that you give the accounts department your new address, so they know where to send your statements," she continued. And on your way out, can you also stop by the legal department to sign some things? I don't get involved in all that," she said as she turned her attention to paperwork on her desk.

He got the message and left. After he signed the papers in Legal without bothering to read them, he left the building permanently. There was no leaving party or fanfare of any kind. He had once been "in" and now he was "out."

As he walked home, he tried to figure out how he was going to live the rest of the year. He would receive his November royalties from Style Raven in a couple of weeks. His next payment after that, his final one, would arrive at the end of December. He needed to find a new job before then. He felt sadder than he had ever felt before. He wished there was somebody he could call. He wished he could go home to Ridgecrest and start over, but he knew that his father wouldn't support him, financially or otherwise. John Webster had always called his son a failure and that was what he had become.

Somehow, he had to make it up to José. It was the only way

to redeem himself. Nothing would bring José back to life but maybe he could help his grandmother. Once he stopped using heroin, he could get a job, put some money aside each week and send it to the grandmother, like José had done. He wished he could get hold of some of his father's money and send it to her. At least she wouldn't have to worry about money. José would have wanted that.

Blake realised he was in front of Sluggo's. Maybe a whiskey would help cheer him up. He hadn't been to Sluggo's since he had stopped going to Blunt.

"Well look who it is." Sluggo said, as Blake entered the bar. "Our most famous customer. Screwdriver?"

"No, give me a whiskey, straight."

As Sluggo poured the whiskey he looked at his friend and noticed his misery.

"You look like shit. What happened?"

"I got fired."

"And?"

"The agency owns my apartment. I have to be out by the end of the month."

"Ouch. I hear there's a vacancy at the Broadway," he joked.

"I wouldn't go back to that dump if they paid me." He took out his wallet to pay for his drink.

"Don't worry about it," Sluggo said, as he made him another. "Both of them are on the house. And you don't even have to tip this time."

* * * * *

Blake felt like the next few weeks went by in slow motion. Or was it fast motion? One night he was sleeping in a luxury flat in Chelsea and the next night he was in his old room at the Broadway. He couldn't be bothered to look for a different place to live. He was too stoned.

He rarely thought about the future anymore. He spent most of his time nodding off in front of whatever film he was watching on his computer at the time. It didn't matter what film it was. He usually couldn't remember it the next day. If he had any thoughts, they were usually about the young model he had killed and his grandmother in the Canary Islands.

Without Phil around, he felt lonely. The only time he went out was to score some dope. Even Carlotta noticed the difference in him. He had become one more failure in a hotel full of failures. He tried to talk to her a few times at the front desk, but she could see by his pinned pupils what the score was. "Just make sure you pay your rent Blake," was all she said.

Carlotta had her own problems. The Turk who had paid for her operation had been busted for a crash and grab of yellow diamonds in the window display of Grafton's. Without him around, she found it difficult dealing with the creeps who owned the hotel. She didn't trust anyone. It seemed like every time Blake went downstairs to score, there were men in grey suits at the desk drawing on paper as if they were planning something. He could care less, as long as it didn't affect him.

* * * * *

Early one evening, Blake was woken up from his nod by a loud knock on his door. He panicked. Nobody knew he was living there. Maybe it was the cops. He quickly hid his works behind his bedside table and went to door.

"Who is it?" he asked.

"Blakey boy! How's it hanging?"

It was Phil. Blake opened the door, grabbed him by his collar, and quickly brought him into the room.

"What the fuck are you doing here? Did Carlotta see you come up?"

"No, no, don't worry, Carlotta didn't see me. She was talking to some of her gangster pals. Chill."

"But how did you know I was living here?"

"I ran into someone from the accounts department at Slick. She told me where you were staying. They mail your statements here."

Phil had actually got the address from his uncle. Carlotta had told Luigi that Blake was staying at the Broadway again.

"So, how's it going?" Phil asked as he straightened his collar. "It's been a while now and nothing has happened, so I thought you'd like a visit."

Blake was sure that Phil's presence could only bring trouble, but he had become so lonely living by himself that he couldn't help but be glad to see his old friend.

"Wanna hit?" he asked Blake. "I just got back from the Hole in The Wall."

"Yeah, Sure."

"I don't have any works, do you? Susan's still on methadone and she doesn't like to have syringes laying around. It's too much of a temptation."

'So that was the real reason for his visit,' Blake thought. 'He needs a place to shoot up.'

Maybe Blake should have thrown him out then, but there was an unwritten code between junkies – they helped each other out when they could - like a family who put aside their past squabbles if one of them was in trouble. An addict might rip another addict off to fund their own habit, but they would also share their cotton, their works or a place to shoot up if one of their junkie brothers or sisters needed it. Blake got his works out from behind the table and an unopened syringe from a bag under the bed, and handed them to Phil. After they were both high, it felt like old times again.

"God, that was good," Phil said, scratching his nose. "So, what are you going to do now that you're not modelling? I thought, maybe, you would go home to clean up. That's what a lot of models from Slick do. You never see them again."

"Are you crazy? When I left home, I said I was never going back, and I meant it."

"But what are you going to do about money? Isn't your dad loaded?"

Blake wished he hadn't told Phil how rich his dad was. It was none of his business.

"I get my last Style Raven cheque at the end of December. Don't know what I'll do after that."

"How old is your dad now?"

"I don't know. I guess he's in his seventies."

"On his last legs, probably."

"Probably."

"Won't you get his money when he dies?"

"No, he's leaving it to a donkey sanctuary."

"A what?"

"A place where they take care of old donkeys. I think it's in the desert near Palmdale."

"What a waste. What about your mother? Isn't she going to get any of the loot?"

"Who knows? I think I already told you that she was only 18 when they got married. She was adopted and her adopted parents wanted to get rid of her. At least that's what the story was in town. He was about sixty at the time. When I was six, she took a load of cash and jewellery from his safe in the attic and left."

"I remember you telling me about the safe. Sounds like quite a bounty."

"It must be worth millions – that stuff in the safe. He's a nutcase. He never spends his money; he just accumulates it."

"Blake, if we could get to that safe and split the loot, we would never have anything to worry about for the rest of our lives. Think about it. And if there was any money after that - insurance money or whatever - we could split that too. I don't believe this stuff about the donkey sanctuary."

As an Italian Phil found it hard to believe that Blake's father had left all of his money to a donkey sanctuary without making a provision for his own flesh and blood. That just wouldn't happen in an Italian family. And then there was the life insurance that his father must have had.

"Did you see the will or insurance papers?" he asked Blake.

"No, of course not. I only know about the safe. But what do you mean, 'think about it?' Think about what?"

"What do I mean? It's easy. He's so old he's probably about to kick the bucket anyway. All he needs is a little push."

"What do you mean by 'a little push'?"

"I mean getting rid of him, Blake."

"Getting rid of him?"

"Yes, getting rid of him. I could take care of it. You wouldn't even need to be involved."

"Are you fucking crazy? He's my father!"

"What the fuck does that matter? What has he ever done for you?"

Blake couldn't answer that question, but Phil's suggestion still made him angry. Didn't he have *any* morals? He wished he hadn't let him in, lonely or not.

"I think you better leave, Phil."

"Ok, ok I'm going. But if your father dies, it probably means all that loot in the safe will either go to the state or a donkey sanctuary. You won't get a cent Blake, from a father who did jack-shit for you."

"Just go Phil. Leave me alone."

"What's one more murder, Blake? It wouldn't be the first time, would it?"

"Get out."

He got out.

What a crap day it had been. Blake nodded off on his bed

and tried to enjoy his high after Phil left, but he couldn't stop thinking of José's poor grandmother. Not only had she lost her grandson, but she would also no longer be getting the money he sent her from New York. Blake compared her to his father. He pictured her going to the market every day with the money José sent her and cooking up a feast for her and her friends. Blake's father cared only about himself. He didn't know how to enjoy life. All he did was save and count and save and count. That wasn't living. He might as well be dead. Maybe Phil was right again.

Blake wasn't the only person thinking about his father. Phil and Susan were having their own discussion about him after Phil arrived home.

"Did you tell Blake about the plan?" Susan asked.

"I suggested it, but he got angry and asked me to leave."

"What are we going to do. Phil? I can't take this anymore. You know when I was a little girl, I always thought I'd be rich when I grew up. I just assumed I would be. Look where I've ended up - living a dead-end life in a cockroach-infested apartment. I've got a degree for god's sake."

It wasn't exactly a degree. It was a certificate for passing a CPR course in high school. And she never even got the certificate. She failed the course. She had a certificate of enrolment.

"Get the father's address and I'll stab him myself if I have to," she said angrily.

"Don't worry baby," her boyfriend responded, "Give it a few days."

16. The Plan

When Blake woke up the next morning, the conversation with Phil was still going through his head. A lot of it hit home. But he would never consider killing his own father. Never. But maybe there was another way. What about blackmail? Phil could threaten to turn his father in to the IRS if he didn't share his loot. Even if his father refused to do it, he wouldn't report Phil to the police because then they would know about the tax evasion. It seemed like a failsafe plan.

There was also a third way that didn't involve a crime. The safest way. The way that most kids got money from their parents. He could call his father and ask for help. That's all he had to do. Swallow his pride and ask for help. He dreaded hearing his father's voice again, but maybe it would be different this time. Maybe his dad missed him, like José's grandmother missed her grandson when he moved to New York. There was no harm in trying.

He had to have a shot of dope, first. He needed to be high to talk to his father. He needed to be high to do anything, nowadays. He went through the ritual of preparing his hit and allowed himself a few minutes after the injection to enjoy its effect before he picked up the phone.

He counted the rings which seemed to go on forever; then there was a click and his father answered. His voice sounded gruff, like he had a problem with his throat: "Hello?" Blake wanted to hang up. "Hello, who is this?" he asked. He sounded angry.

"Dad?"

He waited for a response. Nothing.

"Dad? It's Blake. I... I'm sorry for leaving, Dad. I really am. I'm in New York but I want to come home for a while. Would that be okay?"

"Why?"

"Well, I've kind of fallen on hard times. I was modelling and making a load of money but then that fell through and, well, I just thought it would be nice to come home for a while - to refresh my batteries."

His father answered with a barrage of insults:

"Fuck you, you little shit. What have you ever done for me? It's your fault your mother left. And then *you* left without even warning me. An old man like me. Go to hell, you worthless piece of shit. You're a waste of time. You always have been. I know what you want. Money. Isn't it? Well, you won't get any from me, that's for sure, you failure..."

The voice went on and on. Blake couldn't take it anymore. He hung up and covered his ears. Then he closed his eyes, hoping that would stop the tears that came raining down.

Phil showed up at his hotel a few days later.

"How come you can get to my room without Carlotta even buzzing me?" Blake asked.

"I know Carlotta from way back. Sometimes I feel like I know everybody in New York."

Seeing how friendly Blake was acting, Phil asked him if he had thought about what he said the last time he was there - about his "old man."

Blake brought up the idea of blackmail: "It would be safer than murder."

"Nothing is safe if he's still alive. Who do you think the police are going to believe - a respectable hard-working millionaire like him or his junkie son? Middle-class America would probably find you guilty just for being a model."

"What were you thinking of doing?" Blake was careful to say "you" instead of "we."

"Easy. I take a trip to Crumville, or whatever it's called, in the middle of the night, put the guy out of his misery, and help myself to the treasure. We'll split it when I get back. You stay here and do nothing."

"How are you going to get into the safe?"

"What kind of safe is it?"

"An old one."

"Dial or digital?"

"Dial."

"Dials are a breeze to break into. People think you have to blow up the whole safe. But that's just in the movies. All you really need to do is pry off the dial with a crowbar and unscrew some bits and pieces."

"You might not need to. I might have the combination. I had to do his laundry after mom left and I found a note with some numbers on in one of his pockets. I never used it, but I assumed that it was the combination for the safe: 36-92-66."

"Even better. Either way, there's nothing to worry about. Getting into the safe won't be a problem. Does he keep his tools in the attic? Would he have a crowbar or a drill - tools like that?"

"Yeah, he's got loads of tools up there. He used to be a farmer."

"Great. I forgot about that."

"Are you going to use them to get into the safe if the combination doesn't work?"

"No, I was thinking more of a murder weapon."

Blake felt sick. He wished Phil hadn't used that word. "Murder." It seemed so real. He started to have second thoughts.

"I still don't know about this Phil, what would I have to do?"

"Nothing. You just stay here. You'll have to pay for the flight, of course. And the bus back. I'll take a Greyhound back, so they don't check the luggage."

"You make it sound so easy. I can't believe I'm even listening to you."

"Don't worry so much," Phil said. "People kill people all the time and get away with it. Do you know how many murders the police solve every year? One-third. That means they don't solve two-thirds of them. Did you ever see the movie, *Apocalypse Now*?

"What does that have to do with anything?"

"Look at all the people in Vietnam that were killed by the government. If the U.S. government didn't think there was anything wrong with murder, why should you? Don't think of it as murder. Think of it as putting the guy out of his misery. Even you said that he doesn't enjoy his life. He's going to die regardless of what we do - probably sooner rather than later because of his age. He's not going to know that he's dead when he's dead so what's the big deal? Don't tell me you believe in God."

"What if you get caught?"

"Well, If I get caught before I get to him, it's only 'breaking and entering.' Probably not even a jail sentence. No matter what happens, you'll be safe in New York. It won't have anything to do with you. Once I get back, we can meet on a bench in Bryant Park. I'll put your share of the spoils into a suitcase and leave it in a locker at the Port Authority. I'll give you the key in the park."

"How much money would you need in advance?"

"Just the price of the flight and the bus. And a hotel room in California. Probably about six grand."

"Six grand! That's more than half of my Style Raven cheque

for this month."

"I need to travel first-class. They don't hassle first-class passengers. I'll show you the plane ticket when I get it. I'll get the Greyhound ticket in California. I can sleep on the bus coming back."

"You better not be ripping me off."

"I'm not ripping you off. Okay, give me four grand. I can use your father's money to pay for the bus home if I have to."

"I still don't know if I want to get involved in all this."

"Blake, *you're not involved.* I told you that already. And I'm not going to rip you off. You know where I live, and you know my number. Actually, from now on, you probably shouldn't call me, O.K.? The less people that know I'm in contact with you the better. I'm going to delete you from my phone, and you do the same with me."

Blake walked over to a corner of the room and lifted up part of the carpet. Under it was $2,000. He gave it to Phil. "My private stash."

Phil took it and laughed: "Like father like son."

Blake gave him a dirty look. "Meet me outside the Port Authority tomorrow at 6 pm. I'll give you the rest."

"O.k. I'll be there. Let's see. Today is Thursday. We should move fast. You know that bench in Bryant Park, the one by that big tree on the main pathway to the Hole in The Wall? I'll meet you there next Friday when I'm back. And remember, don't try to contact me on my phone."

* * * * *

The next day Blake was standing outside the Port Authority at 6 pm. No Phil. He walked around for about twenty minutes. Still no Phil. Then, a few minutes later, he saw Susan heading in his direction.

"Blake!"

"What happened to Phil?"

"He asked me to come. Do you have the money?"

"Shhh." Why did she have to be such a loudmouth? There was never an in-between with her. She was either nodding off and completely silent or talking way too loudly.

"Ok, ok, I'll shush. Where's the rest of the money?" she asked in an exaggerated whisper.

He looked around. He didn't want anyone to see him with

her. He stooped down to tie his shoes and left an envelope on the pavement and walked away.

"For fuck's sake," she said as she picked it up. "Hey!" she called after him.

He kept on walking.

"What an asshole," she said to nobody in particular. She peeked in the envelope, saw it was full of cash and practically skipped home.

Blake disappeared among the busy crowds rushing to catch their buses or trains. As he was walking back to the Broadway, he had a horrible feeling that he had made a big mistake. Why did Phil send Susan for the money? How much did she know? Their plan seemed to be falling apart already.

That night his doubts were at least partially allayed when after someone slid a piece of paper under his door that turned out to be a copy of a plane ticket for Filippo Rossi - Phil's real name. The flight was leaving JFK tomorrow, Saturday at 8 am, The plan was going ahead.

Blake had a restless night. No matter how much dope he did, he kept on waking up, wondering if he was doing the right thing. By the morning, he knew he wasn't doing the right thing. He looked at the time on his phone. It was 10 am. Phil was on his way to Los Angeles. There was no way to stop him, now.

An hour later Blake was sweating over a cup of coffee at Gigi's. What had he been thinking of when he agreed to Phil's plan? How could he be so stupid? Things were bound to go wrong, especially with Susan involved. There was nothing to prevent her from going to the cops the next time she had a fight with Phil. It was a dumb idea to begin with. Sure, Blake hated his father but *murder*? He didn't care if Phil kept the money that he gave him, he had to figure out how to stop him. He couldn't call him, but maybe he could get a message to him through the airline. A coded message. Something like "the plans have changed, come home." He could use a fake name and a burner phone and throw it away afterwards. If the police ever got involved, they might suspect it was him, but how could they prove it? And why would the police get involved if the murder never happened...

"Anything wrong?"

Blake looked up and saw Lieutenant Warren standing above him with a paper cup full of coffee.

"No. Nothing. Hi. How are you?"

"Just getting a takeaway for the office. Can I join you instead?"

A cop was the last person Blake wanted to have a coffee with at that moment, but he was afraid that if he said no, Warren might get suspicious. So, instead, he said: "No, of course not. Please, have a seat. I'm not staying that long anyway."

Luigi checked them out from the sandwich counter. He wondered what was going on. He hoped that Phil's name wasn't being mentioned. It had been over a month now since that model's death, but you never knew what a cop like Harry Warren was up to. He remembered how persistent he had been with the Gilman case.

Warren sat down at Blake's table and asked him how things were going.

"What things?"

"I don't know. The modelling, for one."

"It's not going anywhere. Slick dropped me."

"What? How could they drop you? You're the Style Raven guy."

"You know how it is. They're always looking for new faces. My contract with Style Raven ends in December, so Slick let me go."

Lieutenant Warren looked at Blake, at how thin he had become, at how pinned his pupils were and at the bruises on the back of his hands. Only junkies who had run out of veins in their arms had bruises like that. Warren had seen it happen to other people in the fashion business - there was so much dope in New York - but he never thought it would happen to Blake. He felt sorry for him - and angry at the dealers. It wasn't that long ago when Ava was saying how she had to practically beg him to have a glass of champagne.

"Blake, I know you're not a bad guy. Is there anything I can do? What about your father? Have you been in touch with him? Maybe you could go home for a while to... get some rest." He almost said "to clean up."

"My father and I don't get along."

"What about your mom?"

"She left when I was six. I hardly remember her – mostly her blonde hair and her dark red lips. She wore a lot of make-up, even though she never left the house. I think she wanted to be in show business. She used to sing old jazz songs while she did the housework. We would watch musicals together on TV. There was one song – I don't know the name of it – something about facing the music and dancing – that was her favourite. For all I know, she's turning tricks in Times Square, now, with all the rest of the wannabes."

"Why would she be doing that?"

"She married my dad for his money, when she was eighteen. He was about sixty. She couldn't take it after six years and split. Didn't even leave a note."

Warren's heart strings were tugged. He had grown up in similar circumstances.

"I know what you mean," he said. "My dad worked all day and was out most nights drinking or picking up girls. The only adult influence in my life was the neighbourhood cop who treated me like a son. They had neighbourhood cops back then."

"What happened to him?"

"He got knifed by a junkie. That's why I decided to become a cop. Kids raised in the Bronx either became cops or criminals back then - or both."

Warren thought that maybe he could help Blake like that cop who had helped him when he was a kid. Blake felt weird talking to a cop when Phil was on his way to murder his father. He could see Luigi looking at them suspiciously, trying to hear what they were saying. He wondered whether Phil had told him what was going on.

"Maybe I can help you find your mother," Warren suggested. "I could put her name into a computer or something and at least find out where she is. What's her first name?"

Without thinking, Blake answered "Brooke. Her name is Brooke." He wished he hadn't told him as soon as he said it. Now the Lieutenant knew his mother's name. Maybe it didn't matter. It probably wouldn't be difficult to find it out, if Warren didn't know already. His birth certificate must be on record somewhere.

'Well, that was at least something,' Warren thought. 'At least Blake trusted him enough to give him his mother's name.'

"What are you going to do for work?" he asked Blake, hoping to get the conversation going again.

"Who knows?"

"Well, if there's anything I can do, just let me know," Warren said as he stood up to leave. When he got back to the office he typed "Brooke Webster" into the force's criminal database. She had a long history of minor crimes ranging from shoplifting to prostitution. Her last arrest was for soliciting in New Jersey. She'd been working as a topless dancer and got too close to an undercover cop. But that was a few years back and there had been nothing since. No current address or contact details. He checked the obituaries on the internet, but nothing there either. Apart from her arrest records, she didn't exist.

Warren rang Gigi's, thinking that Blake might still be there. He wanted him to know that he had kept his promise about his mother, and to tell him that she was last seen in New Jersey. It wasn't much information, but it would at least show that he was trustworthy; that he did what he said he was going to do. Luigi picked up the phone and said Blake had gone home, back to the Broadway. He asked Warren what was up, but Warren just said it was a social call. 'Why the sudden interest in socialising with Blake?' Luigi wondered.

'So, Blake was back at The Broadway Hotel,' the lieutenant thought. He didn't realise that things were *that* bad for him. At least he knew where Blake was if he needed to get in touch with him again.

After talking to Warren at the restaurant, Blake knew he had to find some way to call off the murder. The cop was on his tail, for whatever reason, and it was making him nervous. On the way back to his hotel room, he bought a cheap burner phone at a magazine shop. He would try to call the airline using a fake name and get a message to Phil that his uncle was ill, and he should come back to New York immediately. Phil would understand. Blake knew the airline wouldn't be able to tell him if Phil was on the flight, but maybe if he pretended to be a limo driver - a fellow worker in the travel industry - the operator might take pity on him. He spoke in a southern accent to further disguise his identity:

"I'm wondering if you can help me ma'am. I'm a limo driver and I'm supposed to be picking up someone at LAX. Filippo Rossi. I can't read my sheet. I think he's flying on MidAir Flight 921. I've had a message from his family that I need to get to him."

"I'm sorry, but I'm not allowed to tell you who is on a flight."

"I know you can't release your passenger list, but couldn't you arrange for one of your staff to give him a message on the plane? I don't want him arriving at the airport thinking that a driver is going to be there when there's not. My boss just called me. There's been a family emergency and he needs to take the next flight back to New York."

Fortunately, he had got an operator at a call centre who hadn't been relieved for her morning break, yet again, and was fed up with her job:

"Look mister, I suppose I can tell you who isn't on the flight, but I can't tell you who *is* on it. He's not on the passenger list. I suppose I can tell you that much. He's not on that flight. Your boss must have given you the wrong information."

"I understand. Maybe he confused him with another passenger. Anyway, thanks for your help."

"You're welcome." She noticed the number on the screen was a New York number. Why would a driver in New York be calling about an L.A. pick-up in a southern accent? She flagged the call, in case it needed to be listened to later, but she didn't have time to be too suspicious. Another call was waiting.

Blake hung up, relieved. So, Phil wasn't even on the flight! He must have faked the photocopy. Blake looked at it again. It looked a real first-class ticket. Maybe he bought the ticket, took the photocopy and then got a refund. Blake didn't care. At least it meant he wasn't on his way to murder his father. He was probably at home with Susan, partying with the money he gave him. Rather than being angry, Blake was relieved. If four grand was the cost of having a live father, then it was worth it. He would still wait for Phil on the bench in Bryant Park next Friday, but he doubted that he would be there. He never wanted to see him again.

Blake took what happened as a sign to start a new life. He would stop using and stick to the straight and narrow; stay away from fashion and get a normal 9 to 5 job like everyone else. But first, he had to score for tonight. He didn't want to get sick. He could always deal with the future, tomorrow.

17. The Attic

Phil and Susan were arriving in L.A. just as Blake was walking down to the Hole in The Wall. Phil had cancelled the flight he was originally booked on and bought two cheaper tickets for him and Susan. She said she needed a holiday, even if it did involve a murder. Couldn't they stop off at Miami on the way home? Phil didn't see why not. It meant that he would miss the appointment on the park bench that he had arranged with Blake, but no big deal. He could explain when he got back since he and Blake had agreed not to call each other.

Susan had managed to get an emergency supply of methadone from her clinic before they left by telling them that her mother had died in Los Angeles, and she needed to be with her family. They didn't ask how someone with such a strong Brooklyn accent happened to have a family in L.A.; they just gave her a two-week supply. She was known for her temper tantrums at the clinic when she didn't get her way and they didn't want to provoke another one. It was too much trouble. They told her she would need to take a blood test when she got back, but she didn't care. She had already decided that she wasn't going back to the clinic. Once Phil and she became millionaires, she wouldn't need it. She would be able to afford heroin. It would be easier to withdraw from heroin (she told herself) because it didn't stay in the body as long as methadone. Besides, she preferred the high.

After arriving in L.A., Susan and Phil took a series of buses to Ridgecrest where they checked into an old budget motel with a couple of suitcases filled with old clothes that they intended to replace with their share of loot from the safe. The rooms were located on two levels outside, with their own entrances. You didn't have to go through reception to get to them, you just had to walk up some rickety wooden stairs. They could come and go as they pleased without being noticed.

Once they unpacked, Susan took a swig from one of her fourteen plastic bottles of methadone – one per day for two weeks – and replaced a red wig she had been wearing since she left the airport with a black one. She had brought five wigs with her, in varying colours, just to confuse any CCTV cameras that might be filming them. She walked down to a Southern Fried Chicken outlet they had noticed on the way to the motel and bought a big tub of chicken, several apple pies (Phil's favourite) and two large fries. Next store was a liquor store where she bought two six packs of XXXtra strength beer. She couldn't resist stealing a couple of Mars bars when the clerk's back was turned. He saw her do it, but didn't particularly care, not on his wages. It was worth it for the cute wink she gave him as she left. He hoped she would be back tomorrow.

After finishing their hefty meal of fried chicken, apple pies, Mars bars and a couple of beers each, Susan and Phil were ready for murder. The motel was within walking distance to Blake's father's house. By the time they left, the streets were so dark that walking to the scene of the crime was probably the safest option; they didn't want to risk taking a cab with a potential witness as a driver. There were no streetlights on the way and the house lights were off in the few homes they passed. It looked like the elderly population of Crumville had all gone to bed, even though it was barely midnight.

"It's so dark, it's scary," Susan commented as she zigzagged down the sidewalk, trying not to bump into Phil.

"Would you be careful?" he said. "You're too out of it."

The combination of beer and methadone had increased the effects of both, and she kept on stepping into the gutter by mistake.

"Who would want to live here?" she slurred. "It's like being in a scary movie."

When they got near to the father's house, Phil handed her a pair of black latex gloves he had picked up in a sex shop in Manhattan.

"We don't want to leave fingerprints," he explained.

"This is so exciting!" she said, giggling as she put them on, like she was getting ready for a murder mystery weekend.

They stood looking up at Blake's father's house. There was only one light on in a room at the very top.

"Must be the attic," Phil deduced intelligently. Blake had drawn them a map of the house and the room was clearly labelled "attic" in his handwriting. Phil considered breaking into the back of the house, but it seemed like too much trouble. Instead, he inserted his bank card into the space between the door and doorframe and forced the latch open. He was surprised that it opened so easily. Phil's father had forgot to lock the deadbolt from inside. "That's small-town America for you," he said to Susan. She squeezed his arm in excitement and wished she was as smart as him. She didn't even know where north and south was, let alone able to read a map. She only knew "uptown" and "downtown."

Following Blake's map, Phil guided Susan up the stairs, checking out each room as they passed in order to make sure nobody was in it. At one point, Susan opened a hallway closet and found a collection of Luis Vuitton luggage. "This must be worth a fortune," she said as she helped herself to one big bag and a clutch purse. Phil bleated – they already had two suitcases with them – but when she told him how much they were worth – "tens of thousands" – he changed his mind.

"They must have belonged to Blake's mom," Susan said. "What a nice woman she must have been. If this is what she left behind when she split, there must be tons of expensive stuff lying around."

"Susan. We need to stay focused," Phil whispered, pointing to the closed door at the top of the stairs. "He's in there, probably counting his loot." They could see light seeping out from the bottom of the door.

When they arrived outside the door, Phil told Susan to stay in the hallway with their empty suitcases while he went in. Things could get violent. Adrenalin started rushing through his body as he pushed the door open slightly, hoping that Blake's father wouldn't be facing it. He knew that once he was in the room, he would have to move fast to find a murder weapon - something he could hit Blake's father on the head with. He pushed the door further and further, until it was completely open. Blake's father was in the room, but he didn't react to his visitor's presence.

"What's wrong?" Susan asked, as she peeked over Phil's shoulder. "Oh my god! That's disgusting!"

Blake's father was hanging by a rope attached to a ceiling pipe, swaying above an overturned wooden stool. He was naked except for a pair of stained y-fronts. A large selection of pornography was spread out on the floor beneath him - mostly pictures of women who were, like him, hanging by a noose, or tied to iron crosses while being whipped and tortured by their "masters." Some had tit clamps attached to their nipples with weights hanging from them and ball gags in their mouths. A few had been used as human ashtrays, judging from the burn scars on their bodies. Others were urinating as they were tortured, their eyes opened wide with fear.

"He must have been into autoerotic asphyxiation," Phil said

matter-of-factly.

"What the fuck is that?" Susan asked.

"It's when you hang yourself while you're jacking off. Cutting off the oxygen supply temporarily makes you feel high. But you're supposed to stop before you die. He must have kicked the stool over while he was struggling with the noose."

"That's creepy."

"Some people really like it. Wanna try?" Phil started chasing Susan around the room, laughing.

"Get away from me!" she yelled, playfully.

They ran around the hanging body like kids playing tag until Phil noticed the open safe. Thick stacks of bills cushioned what appeared to be a limitless assortment of gold coins and jewellery.

"C'mon," Phil said. "We better hurry up. We need to fill those suitcases."

They filled their cases with as much bounty as they could, and Phil told Susan to take them downstairs.

"But they're so heavy," she complained, like a petulant child.

"Drag them."

"Why? What are you going to do? The guy is already dead."

"I know. But we have to make it look like we killed him. Otherwise, Blake might think we don't deserve our cut."

It wasn't just the spoils from the safe that Phil was worried about; Blake had also promised him a cut from any future money – donkey sanctuary or not. If Blake's dad had life insurance, the insurance company might not pay out if they thought their client had hung himself by choice.

It was also a question of control. Phil got off on controlling people. He controlled Susan through her addiction and Blake through his involvement in the murder of his father. Without a murder, Phil would lose that control. Blake might not keep his mouth shut. Although initially, Phil had assured Blake that "he wasn't involved," he would make it clear when he got back that Blake was very much involved. He had provided his father's address, a key to the front door, a handwritten map of the house and even the combination to the safe.

Susan looked at the hanging body. "What are you going to do to it?" she asked.

"Don't worry your pretty little head about that. Just take the bags downstairs."

She dragged the suitcases down the stairs, step by step, while

Phil looked at the hanging body and tried to figure out what to do next. Blake's father looked so small - just a frail old man - not at all like the ogre Blake had characterised him as. Phil almost felt sorry for him. All the old guy was doing was trying to have fun; so what if he was a little perverted? He wished he had a relative with interests like that. His Uncle Luigi was probably the same age as Phil's dad, but he was so boring - all he did was complain about life. Even Phil was getting a hard-on from seeing the magazines on the floor.

'Oh well, gotta do what I have to do' he said to himself as he noticed a drill and a pair of gardening shears on a worktable.

He put the stool upright and stood on it to cut the noose with the shears. The body fell with a thud on the floor. He dropped the shears on the floor and got the drill, turned it on and drilled through the father's face. It wasn't as easy as he expected. He kept on hitting bone. 'Cheap fucking drill,' he complained as he tossed it aside.

He picked up the shears and tried to use one of the blades to detach the head from the body, but it was too clumsy - like trying to decapitate someone with a giant pair of scissors. He was afraid of cutting himself with the other end of the shears and he didn't want to leave any traces of his blood that could be found later by the police. He noticed a shovel leaning against the wall and grabbed that. Using the edge of the shovel as an axe, he chopped at the father's neck until his head was almost detached. He eventually gave up. Thick blood was gurgling from the neck, and he didn't want to get any of it on himself. He wondered how long Blake's father had been dead. The blood was so thick that it was oozing out like red lava instead of liquid.

"I'm afraid that's the best I can do," he said to Blake's father. It was weird talking to a dead body. Its eyes were still open.

He left the shovel on the floor and went downstairs to join Susan who was waiting by the front door with the suitcases. They walked back to the hotel with their bounty and went straight to their room.

"Murder has never been easier!" Phil joked when they emptied the contents of the suitcases on the bed. Susan could barely contain her excitement. She loved Phil, she told herself. She really did.

There was one slight problem that they weren't aware of. Sounds from the attic tended to travel to the lower floors and even to the next-door neighbour's house where an elderly couple lived. They were in bed when Phil and Susan were in the attic. The husband was asleep, but his wife was wide awake, lying next to him reading a book a friend had loaned her. It was a new account of the Charles Manson murders that took place in the '60s when she was a young girl. She loved a good murder. Just as she got to the part where Patricia Krenwinkel was stabbing Abigail Folger on Sharon Tate's front lawn, she thought she could hear the sound of a drill next door.

"Mr. Webster is up late," she commented to her sleeping husband. "Do you hear drilling?" she asked. "No," he mumbled before turning over so he could get back to sleep.

She eventually got up and looked out the bedroom window. She didn't see anything particularly suspicious, just a young couple with suitcases further down the road, walking toward the Travelodge. She wished she could be part of a young couple again. Then she went back to bed.

18. Mission Accomplished

On Friday night of the following week, Blake sat on the bench at 10 pm where he and Phil had agreed to meet as part of their plan. Phil's absence didn't surprise him; it was just further confirmation that he hadn't gone through with the plan.

Phil wasn't there because Susan and him were busy getting drunk at a gay resort in Miami where they decided to spend a few days on their way back to New York. Susan even managed to score some smack in the seedier section of town with money from the safe and Phil got his hands on some crystal meth in a gay disco. Staying at a gay resort was perfect for both of them. Susan "loved" gay people (she never stopped telling them when she was drunk) and Phil loved the fact that straight guys weren't trying to hit on her. He didn't mind that some of them flirted with him. In New York, nobody flirted with him, male or female.

Blake waited on the bench in Bryant Park for about half an hour before he gave up and went back to the Broadway. He had been to the Hole in The Wall earlier that day and had scored enough smack to last him for a week. By Monday, most of it was gone. The initial relief he felt when he thought that Phil had ripped him off, was also gone. He could use that money. He still had some money in the bank and was expecting his two last transfers from Style Raven in the next couple of months, but what was he supposed to do when that was gone? His anger increased every time he came to the end of yet another bag of smack. He was amazed at how quickly he got through the stuff. He could remember the days when half a bag would get him through an entire day; now he needed at least two.

He considered calling Phil on his phone and giving him a hard time. What did it matter if his number was on his phone if he hadn't gone through with the murder? Maybe the best thing would be to visit him in person. That might be dangerous, but there was a pawnshop downstairs that sold switchblades. He had fooled around with them when he was a kid. Maybe he should get one for his own protection. As he sat on his bed wondering what to do, somebody knocked on his door. 'Probably that lieutenant' he thought. That guy was really becoming a nuisance. He wished he hadn't told him about his mother. He opened the door.

"Hey buddy! I'm back!"

It was Phil, standing there with a suitcase. Blake grabbed him by the collar and brought him into the room. "Listen you bastard...." he started to say, but Phil told him to "wait a sec" and dragged the suitcase into the room. Blake thought that he had a lot of nerve. He wondered if Phil had split up with Susan and he needed a place to stay.

"Mission accomplished!" Phil announced, as he unlocked the suitcase.

"What do you mean, 'Mission accomplished?'" Blake asked angrily.

"I hate to break the bad news to you my friend but that mother-fucking rich bastard of a father of yours is dead." He wiped away some non-existent tears. "And this, my friend, is all yours." He opened the suitcase and a torrent of cash and jewellery cascaded onto the floor.

"I tried to divvy it up equally, but I'm not exactly a gold expert. The rest of the stuff is at my house."

Blake could barely get his words out. "But I rang the airline. You weren't on the flight."

"Nah, it was all last minute. You know what Susan is like. She wanted to combine the trip with a few days of holiday in Florida. I cashed in the first-class flight and got cheaper ones for both of us. We spent a couple days in Miami on the way back."

The reality of what had happened sunk in as Phil told him in detail about how they had killed his father. He laughed as he said, "You should have heard his bones cracking. It's not easy to drill through somebody's head you know..." He didn't mention that Blake's father was already dead by the time they got to him.

Blake threw up in the sink in his room. He stared at Phil from the mirror above the sink: "You killed my father, Phil, you killed him."

Phil responded angrily: "No Blake, you killed your father. We might have done the dirty work, but you were the one who was ultimately responsible. We just did what you told us to do, so don't fucking blame us for what happened. I actually felt sorry for the guy."

When Blake didn't respond, Phil continued, "Besides, nobody will ever know except for you and me and Susan. Don't worry about getting rid of the jewellery. I know tons of pawnshops that will take stuff without asking questions."

Blake turned to face Phil: "You have to leave, Phil, and we

have to never see each other again."

"I'll leave for now, but remember I get a cut of anything else that comes in. That was the deal."

"Did Carlotta see you come in?"

"The front desk was empty," he lied.

"What about Susan?"

"Susan won't say anything. I can take care of Susan. She wanted you to have this."

He threw three small bottles of methadone onto the bed. "They're what's left from Susan's allocation. She's not going back to the clinic. She can afford the real thing now. I was going to sell them, but I don't really need the money. You might as well have them."

"Just leave Phil. Please."

"I'll leave, but don't forget your promise."

"Don't worry, you'll get what you deserve."

Phil knew he would get whatever he was owed out of any future income as long as Blake was under his control - as long as Blake remained scared that Phil might go to the police and say that Blake was the person who planned the whole thing. Even if Blake managed to escape his clutches, Phil had still made a considerable amount out of him. He had split their spoils three ways. Blake got a third and Phil got two thirds. He thought it was only fair because he was part of a couple. Susan would get that millionaire lifestyle she craved as soon as he got rid of some of the jewellery.

As Phil passed the front desk on his way out of the hotel, Carlotta did what she had done when he came in. She pretended to be looking at the reservations book. He had carte blanche of the hotel because of his connection to Luigi and Luigi's connection to the people who owned the hotel. But she didn't want to get involved in his shit. Hear no evil, speak no evil, see no evil.

Blake made the decision that night to leave. He would book a flight tomorrow for the Canaries to find José's grandmother. It was the only way to redeem himself. He finished off the one bag he had left and fell asleep. He would stop by the Hole in the Wall for the final time tomorrow when he went to book his ticket.

* * * * *

While Phil and Blake were having their conversation at the Broadway, Lieutenant Warren and his boss were discussing the same murder at their office, about three blocks from the hotel. The body had been found by the Ridgecrest police after John Webster's bank manager became concerned when his elderly client hadn't shown up for an appointment.

The cops met the manager at the Webster house; Phil and Susan had left the door unlocked and it didn't take long for them to find the body. The Ridgecrest cops contacted the Kern County cops who called in forensics. They also emailed a set of gruesome photos to Captain Seligman after finding out that the NYPD had had contact with Webster's son previously. Seligman called in Warren.

"Are the county police saying the father was murdered?" Warren asked when he arrived in Seligman's office and saw the photos.

"What do you think?" the captain answered. "It's not easy to decapitate yourself."

"What about prints?"

"Who knows? Forensics have dusted the whole house and they're photographing the prints now. So far all they've come up with is Mr. Webster's fingerprints and an empty safe. The body wasn't in great shape when they found it. He'd been dead for a while. The front door wasn't even locked."

"A robbery gone bad?"

"Might be."

Warren looked closer at the photographs, hoping to discover a clue of some sort. Seligman asked if he had ever heard of autoerotic asphyxiation.

"Isn't that teenager stuff? There was that story in the press recently about that actor's brother who died doing it. You don't think Blake's father was into it, do you? Wasn't he in his seventies?"

"Don't be an ageist," Seligman responded with more than a hint of sarcasm. "They found a noose near the body. Palmdale thinks that maybe the thieves got lucky; that John Webster was already dead when they arrived."

"Why the bashed-in face?"

"Who knows? It's what you call a mystery. Kern County is still waiting for the forensics report. Although they haven't done a full autopsy yet, the medical examiner is saying that the wounds were inflicted sometime between noon and midnight over a week ago – not last Saturday but the one before that. Whether or not the wounds actually caused the death is another story. You wouldn't happen to know where Blake was on that day, would you?

"I can ask him, but I doubt if he'd be capable of doing something like that."

"Check out his schedule with Slick."

"He doesn't work for Slick anymore. He got dropped."

"Why?"

"Not sure. He says they need a new face, but he looked strung out to me."

"So, he needs money?"

"Probably."

"His father was very rich man. He left his money to a donkey sanctuary that got busted about a month ago. It was a scam. So, either Blake or his mother will get the money."

"I tried to find his mother at one point. No luck. She was busted in a topless joint in New Jersey a while ago, but then she disappeared from the radar. Nothing. It's weird. How can a person just vanish like that?"

"Well, we need to tell Blake about his father's death anyway. Why don't you pay him a visit?"

"Sure, why not?"

"See if he has an alibi."

"No problem."

"A confession would be even better."

"A confession?"

"You never know," Seligman said, putting away the pictures. "And Harry, this could get serious. I'll give you free rein for the moment, but don't do anything stupid. Don't try to be a hero. Whatever happens with this case, I still think you should resign. The offer still stands."

"Thanks, but no thanks."

19. The Blonde Next Door

Usually when Blake had a hit, it dampened down his nightmares. But this time it didn't work. He dreamt he was outside Blunt, except it wasn't Blunt, it was a circus big top. Eloise was there with her clipboard, facing the inside of the tent, except it wasn't Eloise. When she turned around, he saw that it was his father; at least his father's head was on top of Eloise's body. He was smiling, encouraging Blake to come forward using one of Eloise's arms as his own. His lips were moving in slow motion - it looked like he was mouthing the words, 'come join the fun.' Then 'fun' became 'fail' and it looked like he was saying 'come fail' as his face moved closer and closer, sucking Blake into the darkness of his mouth. The darkness became Nelson's Room. Jose's grandmother was sitting at a small table, giving a puppet show. Except they weren't puppets. They were miniature versions of Phil and Susan. They were alive but her hands were inside of them, making them wave frantically at Blake. Then, suddenly, his father's lips snapped shut like a mousetrap and cockroaches flowed from the corners of his mouth. Blake woke up screaming. It felt like the roaches were in bed with him. Sweat was pouring down his face.

He needed another hit. The spoon he used earlier was on the bedside table with the cotton still in it. His syringe sat in a glass next to a bottle of water. He quickly added water to the spoon, sucked the liquid through the cotton and into the barrel of the syringe. He slapped the back of his hand to make the veins stand out and then stabbed one with the needle. He pressed the plunger up and down a few times to get every last bit of leftover dope. He didn't have to wait long to feel the effect. It wasn't much, but it did the job. He fell back asleep, and the nightmares disappeared.

The next morning, he woke up to someone making a racket in the hallway outside his room. He looked at his watch - thanks to his father (and Phil), he now had a watch - a Rolex Submariner - worth more than $20,000 of tax-free income. It wasn't even 8 am yet. He wondered if the cops were outside. Maybe Susan had squealed, and they were coming to arrest him. He told himself he didn't care anymore, but he did - there was just nothing he could do about it. He thought about jumping out the window, but it was so small he doubted he would fit. He had no choice but to let them arrest him. He got out of bed and opened his door slightly, just enough to peek into the hallway. Instead of cops, he saw a leggy blonde fumbling with her key card. He opened the door wider.

"What's going on?" he asked

"Oh, I'm so sorry, I've just moved in – or am trying to, at least. I can't get the key card to work."

He laughed. "Hold on." He realised he was in his boxer shorts and quickly slipped into a pair of jeans that were on the floor next to his bed.

'A new neighbour,' he thought – an older woman but still sexy - with blue eyes like him. It was difficult to tell just how old she was because of all the make-up she was wearing – anywhere between thirty to fifty. She looked sort of familiar - he wondered if he had seen her before, maybe when he used to cruise the hookers in Times Square.

"Here, let me help you." He took the card and rubbed it against the door to get the dents out. It worked this time.

She laughed at how simple it was. Then they just stood there in silence, staring into each other's blue eyes.

"Sorry," she said, as if she had just come out of trance. "Thank you so much for getting the key to work."

"Do you need help with your bags?"

"Oh yes, if you don't mind. that's very nice of you." she said in such a gentle voice that he had second thoughts about her profession. She seemed too polite to be a hooker. But when he knelt down to pick up one of her bags, he noticed her scuffed stilettos and torn lace stockings.

"I know this sounds like a strange question," she said when they were in her room, "but have I met you before? You look familiar."

"I used to be a model," he answered, feeling embarrassed. "The Style Raven guy."

"Oh, of course, that must be it. Style Raven. I had a boyfriend who used their shaving cream. You look different now."

"It's been a difficult year."

"Well, thank you for your help. I'll see you later, probably."

"Yeah – 'ships in the night.'"

When she looked puzzled, he explained, "My mother used that expression. It's from a movie, but don't ask which one."

"I'm a big movie freak too."

She walked him out to the hallway, thanking him again for his help. He turned away from her to go back to his room and then kept on turning until he was facing her again: "Hey, I've just had an idea. I hear there's a party in room no. 9 tonight."

She looked at the numbers on the doors. "But that's your room."

"Why, so it is," he said. "How about it?" Normally, he wasn't so brazen, but tonight was his last night in New York. Although his rent was paid until the end of his month, he wasn't sure when he would be back, if ever. He was leaving for the Canaries tomorrow. He didn't want to spend his last night in New York on his own. Besides, he was turned on by her torn stockings. He hadn't been with a woman for a long time.

"Sure." she answered. "How could a girl say no to a style raven? Oh god, I'm beginning to sound like a commercial!" They laughed.

"Is 8:00 okay?" he asked.

"Sure. Why not? I'll see you tonight," she said as she went back into her room, locking the door behind her. He stood in the hallway long enough to overhear her talking to a friend on her phone saying she had a date with the "Style Raven guy."

He hadn't told her that the "party" was a going away party for himself. He felt good about what he was doing. Giving José's grandmother a cut of the spoils wouldn't bring her grandson back, but it would at least make up for the money that he used to send her. She would never need to know where the money came from. Once he had her address, he could leave a package on her porch or mail it to her. He remembered that José had said he lived with her near some place called the Yumbo Centre and her name was Luisa Fernandez. It shouldn't be too difficult to find her. Blake's father would have at last, however unknowingly, done a good deed.

His reasons for the trip weren't entirely charitable. He remembered what José had told him about the Canaries not having an extradition treaty with the U.S. If Susan or Phil squealed, he would at least be safe for the time being. He planned on making a booking today for a flight tomorrow morning if there was one. He'd leave some of his bounty in a locker at the Port Authority for when he came back, but he'd take as much as he could with him without attracting too much attention from Customs.

He could probably hide most of the grandmother's share in

the pockets of clothes in his luggage. There were two other Rolexes, each worth about twenty grand and other jewellery worth hundreds of thousands of dollars. He could wear a lot of it and even if his bags were inspected by Customs, it probably wasn't that unusual for a first-class passenger to travel with an assortment of jewellery. Some of the jewellery was in the form of solid gold belt buckles that wouldn't be noticed if they were attached to belts.

He also wanted to take Susan's methadone so he wouldn't get sick. If he took it carefully, in small amounts, he could use it to take the edge off his withdrawals. Nobody would notice it among his toiletries disguised as a bottle of cologne.

After stuffing two shopping bags full of leftover cash and stolen goods into a locker at the Port Authority for when he got back to New York, he booked a flight with Air Morocco that left JFK early tomorrow morning and arrived at Las Palmas airport Friday morning, with a stopover in Casablanca. He'd have to travel using his real passport, with his real name, but the trip would at least buy him some time. He wondered how long it would take for someone to find his father's body, not knowing that they already had. He didn't want to think about it. The important thing was to find José's grandmother.

He stopped by the Hole in The Wall on the way home. He planned on making his last night in New York a good one. He didn't want to be clucking during his date with his neighbour and he didn't want to dip into Susan's methadone until he reached the Canaries. Everything was working out perfectly - until things started to go wrong.

When he knocked two times on the door of the Hole in The Wall, like you were supposed to, nothing happened. The peephole stayed closed. He tried it again, but he still didn't get a response. He looked around and couldn't see any spotters. It looked like the Hole in The Wall was no longer in operation.

He didn't know what to do. He didn't want to hang around in case it had been busted. He started to walk back to his hotel. As he was going through Bryant Park, someone passed him and mumbled "You 'lookin'?" in barely a whisper. Blake recognised him as one of the spotters and caught up with him. They had a quick conversation without looking at each other, as they walked along.

"What happened to the Hole in The Wall?" Blake asked.

"It got busted. Want something?"

"Yeah."

"How many?"

"Two."

"Money."

The deal took place like a dance by participants who knew by instinctively what to do; they didn't have to be taught the steps. Blake had already crumpled up some bills in his pocket while they were talking. A fistful of money met the open palm of the spotter without anybody else in the park noticing. The spotter then sat down on a nearby bench until Blake passed in front of him. When the spotter got up and walked in the opposite direction, there were two glassine envelopes on the bench. Blake sat down, retrieved them, and walked quickly home, holding the envelopes in his closed palm so he could drop them if any cops approached. Halfway to his hotel, he decided it was safe enough to put them in his pocket.

Scoring openly like that was always a risk, but Blake needn't have worried. The cops had been to the Hole in The Wall last the night before, though they didn't want to bust the place at all. They would have preferred it to remain open and under surveillance. But after numerous complaints by Mr. and Mrs. Gentrification about the shady people hanging out near the building, they had no choice but to make a token bust. The only people who got arrested were some of the spotters, but the force made it look like a big thing – police cars, a van and sirens - so that the locals knew they were doing their job and would stop complaining to the City Council that the cops weren't doing anything about the drug dealing in the neighbourhood.

The officers interviewed the spotters back at the station but didn't get much information, nor did they expect to. One spotter told a cop about an overdose he had witnessed in the alley, but the cop hadn't heard about José's case and wasn't particularly concerned. There was no reason he should have been. The case had already been closed as an accidental overdose. The only person who was still agonising over it, was Blake.

When Blake arrived back at the Broadway with a pocketful of heroin, he noticed that Carlotta was talking to someone at the front desk. Lieutenant Warren. Damn. Blake tried to leave the way he came but Carlotta had already seen him.

"There. You see," she said to Warren. "I knew he'd be back soon. He's never gone for long."

"What's up?" he asked Warren, as casually as possible given

the circumstances.

"I need to talk to you about something." Warren said. "But not here. Can we go up to your room?"

He couldn't remember if he had left his works out.

"My room's a mess right now."

"Would you prefer to go back to my office?" When he saw the expression on Blake's face, he suggested a coffee at Gigi's instead.

"Okay. But I don't have much time. I need to clean my room."

"It won't take a long time Blake, but I really do need to talk to you. It's about your father." Blake's face hardened. Carlotta pretended not to be listening.

"What about my father?"

"Let's go to Gigi's."

They went to Gigi's and ordered some coffees and panini. Luigi took their order and listened to as much of their conversation as he could when he went back to the sandwich counter. Warren held on to Blake's arm and looked directly at his eyes: "I'm really sorry to have to break this news to you, but your father is dead."

He watched carefully to see how Blake reacted. A son's normal reaction to the death of his father usually involved tears, but murderers reacted differently. They tried to find out how much the police knew.

"How did it happen?" Blake asked, tearless.

"We don't have all the details yet. Sorry about this Blake, but I need to get an idea of your whereabouts the Saturday before last."

"My whereabouts? Why would you ask that? Do you mean he was murdered?

"Not sure. Where were you, Blake?"

"Two Saturdays ago?"

"That's what I said."

"With you."

"Huh?"

"We shared sob stories here at Luigi's. I told you about my childhood, about my mom. You told me about your cop friend being stabbed. You said you would look for my mom. Remember?"

Warren was embarrassed at not having remembered.

"That was Saturday afternoon, what about Saturday night or

Sunday morning?" he asked.

"Are you really suggesting that after I saw you, I flew to L.A. and murdered my own father?"

"I'm sorry Blake. I suppose it is a stupid question. To be honest, my boss wanted me to ask you and I completely forgot that it was on that day that we had our conversation. He wants me to retire. Maybe he's right."

"Tell your boss I was in my room. Carlotta will vouch for that. But, please, tell me what happened to my father. Was he murdered?"

Warren doubted that Carlotta would vouch for anything, especially in court.

"Blake, I can't answer that yet. We're still waiting for the Kern County cops to get back to us."

They sat in silence. Warren decided to try the sympathy angle again. So far, there hadn't been any tears. "I just wanted to say I'm sorry, Blake. About your father. I really am. I know you said before that you didn't get along with him, but still, a father's death is a pretty big thing. You must have had some feelings for him."

"You're right, I did have a feeling for him. Hatred. I hated his guts."

That complicated things. Although Blake's lack of tears might normally be considered suspicious, the fact that he was so open about hating his father put a new slant on things. Maybe he was telling the truth, after all.

Warren continued: "You know, by dying, he might have made you a millionaire."

"What do you mean?" Blake asked cautiously. Warren hadn't mentioned the safe yet.

"Your father was a very rich man, Blake. Very rich."

"He told me he was leaving all his money to a donkey sanctuary."

"He did. But it was a scam. The 'charity' got busted about a month ago. They no longer exist. So, his money goes to his heirs. His wife and you. Except we can't find the wife."

If what Lieutenant Warren said was true, Phil had been right. There was a good possibility that there would be more money in the future. He would make sure Phil got his cut. But it wouldn't stop him from going to the Canaries to find José's grandmother. He would make sure she would get a cut of any additional money, too.

"Here, take this." The lieutenant handed him a piece of paper. "It's the contact details of your father's lawyer. You should get in touch with him. When was the last time you spoke to your father?"

"I rang him after moving back into the Broadway. I asked if I could come back home for a rest, until I sorted things out."

"What 'things'?"

"The agency dropping me. Stuff like that."

"And what did he say?"

"What he always said - that I was a loser."

"I'm sorry. How did it make you feel? Angry?"

"If you're suggesting that I murdered my father out of anger, I already gave you an alibi."

"You seem pretty sure it was murder."

"How the fuck would I know? I wasn't involved."

"What weren't you involved in?"

"In nothing. Can we continue this conversation tomorrow? I want to clean my room before tonight. Believe it to not, I've got a date."

"Yeah, sure. Why don't I stop by about 4:00 tomorrow afternoon? We should have heard back from forensics by then."

"O.K, fine." Blake answered, knowing that he would already be on his flight to freedom by then.

20. The Date

Blake sat in his room nodding off, waiting for his date. He hoped she liked whiskey. He had bought a bottle of Jim Beam which sat on the bedside table next to two plastic tumblers. A bag of ice and bottle of coke were in the sink, in case she wanted a mixer.

After cleaning his room, he had packed his suitcases and treated himself to a large hit of dope that would last him all night. Even though his flight didn't leave until the morning, he was going to take a taxi to the airport as soon as his neighbour left. He probably should never have invited her over, but it seemed like a good idea at the time. Every minute he stayed in that hotel room he risked being visited by cops. Now that they had discovered his father's body it was just a matter of time before they put two and two together.

He hoped his date wouldn't be "fashionably" late. When he was a model, he was usually so worried about being late that he showed up early. Everybody else was late. 'When I was a model...' he repeated to himself. It seemed like such a long time ago. The more he thought about it, the more depressed he became. He poured himself a whiskey, straight, and continued to wait.

At exactly 8:00, he heard her door open and close. Thank God she was on time. She tapped on his door a few times and he opened it with a broad smile on his face – his model's smile – and invited her in to his "palace." He offered her the one chair in the room and asked if a whiskey and coke was okay.

"Perfect," she said. When she sat down Blake noticed that her dress was so short that she had to cross her legs to hide what was under it. He wondered if she was wearing any underwear. It was a black dress but different than the one she was wearing when they first met. Her black stockings were different too. They were new. No rips. It was like she had made an extra effort to look good now that she knew he was the "Style Raven guy." He worried that she was going to be disappointed as he handed her a drink.

"Thanks," she said, her eyes sparkling with admiration, like she was dating a 'star.' It only made Blake more depressed. He noticed that she barely sipped the drink whereas he was gulping his down. She set hers down on the bedside table, next to the bottle. Blake noticed the heavy imprint she left on the tumbler with her dark red lipstick and felt turned on.

"You've hardly had any," he remarked.

"I like to take it slow," she answered. "I'm meeting some girlfriends later."

He was happy to hear that. Maybe she would leave early. As the minutes ticked by, he was becoming increasingly worried that he would be arrested at any time. He kept looking at his watch.

"Hey, where are you? Got something on your mind?" his date asked.

"No," he said too quickly. "Why do you ask?

"I don't know. Your mouth is smiling, but not your eyes."

"I was just daydreaming."

"At night? On a date?"

"My agency dropped me," he said, hoping that might explain his mood.

"Why?"

"Oh, you know. They're always looking for the next new look, the next new face. I wasn't new anymore. But what about you? What's your story? I don't even know your name."

She laughed. "My friends call me Blondine," she said as she fluffed up her blonde hair. "O.k., it's not my natural colour, but I've been blonde for so long I don't even remember my natural colour."

He liked her down-to-earth honesty. "What do you do?" he asked. "It seems like most people in his hotel are either drug addicts, alcoholics or criminals. Which one are you?"

"None of the above. I used to be a middle school teacher, but my husband wasn't a nice man. I left and came here. I'm sort of 'in hiding,' although some friends know where I'm at. I guess I'm a battered girlfriend. But I'm making the best of it." She raised her glass as if to make a toast. "To freedom," she said.

"Yeah, freedom," Blake said, and poured himself another drink. He didn't believe for an instant that she had been a middle school teacher. A middle school teacher wouldn't have known about this hotel. A middle school teacher wouldn't own such a sexy dress. In his drunken state, the shortness of it and the way it showed off her cleavage made it seem more like an invitation than a dress. He had probably been right all along. 'She must a prostitute' he thought. 'Maybe trying to escape from her pimp.' The girls he picked up on Times Square used to talk about how horrible their pimps were, but they always went back to them, even when he offered them a place to stay.

He sat down on the bed, trying to remember if he was on his third or fourth drink. She was still nursing her first.

"Drink up," he slurred. "It might make you feel better. I'm on your side."

"Thanks. I appreciate the support."

They sat in silence, neither knowing what to say next. Then she stood up like she was going to leave, and he felt like an empty pit had formed in his stomach. He should have been relieved, but all he felt was needy and helpless. He didn't know whether he wanted her to leave or stay.

"Please, stay for a while," he said, slurring his words because of all the alcohol and dope. "I know you have to meet your girlfriends but, to be honest, I could use some human comfort. It sounds like you probably could, as well. Here, sit here." He padded the bed next to him.

She sat down. He handed her drink to her.

"I've been through a lot lately," she said, "and I don't want to be an imposition."

"Don't worry. You're not an imposition. It's not like I've got things to do, or anything."

He could smell her perfume. Expensive. Some of the models used to wear it. He was confused. It was classy - not the type of perfume that a prostitute would wear. They tended to go for cheap, strong-smelling stuff.

He put his arm around her shoulders. To his surprise, she leaned her head against his chest. He caressed her hair lightly. She looked up and smiled. Her dark red lips looked so inviting against her pale skin that he couldn't help kissing them. She didn't move away, but neither did she return the kiss. He tried again. This time she opened her lips, inviting him in.

Slowly, they fell back on the bed. He lay on his side next to her. His hand seemed to move by its own volition. He pulled her short dress up and pulled down a pair of red lace panties. He threw them on the floor and started to massage her with his finger. She moaned. He pulled down his jeans and underwear and got on top of her.

"I really shouldn't be doing this," she said.

"Why not?" he asked.

"I, I," she stammered like she wanted to tell him something, but ended up just saying, "it's too soon."

She didn't resist as he continued. It wasn't long before he was inside her with her dress pulled up to her waist, the sweat from his face falling on her neck as he pushed into her harder and harder. She gasped as though she was in pain, or pleasure. They breathed in rhythm with each other. Then she moaned loudly as he came inside her. He continued the pressure, using his cum as a lubricant, and she came shortly after him. Then it was over. He withdrew and laid on his back beside her. It had happened so quickly.

"I'm sorry," he said, "I didn't expect that to happen."

"I didn't say no, did I?"

He laughed. "No, you didn't say no."

It was true that she hadn't said no, but she looked worried. He wondered what was going through her mind. She was probably wondering the same thing about him - why he looked so worried. He liked her. She reminded him of him.

"Do you mind if I smoke?" he asked.

"No, of course not."

He took a cigarette from the pack in his jeans on the floor and offered her one, which she accepted. He took an ashtray from the bedside table and put it between them on the bed. She pulled down the bottom of her dress to cover her crotch and he pulled up his jeans. They both lay there in silence. He enjoyed the silence. He enjoyed the luxury of lying next to a woman without feeling the need to say anything. It didn't matter how old she was - or maybe that's why he felt so comfortable.

When he finished his cigarette, he stood up to get another drink and almost fell over. He couldn't remember how many drinks he had. Holding onto the sink, he poured himself another whiskey. Her still unfinished drink sat on the corner of the sink.

As he poured his whiskey, he saw from his watch that it was after 11 pm. He wanted to leave soon for the airport. She noticed him looking at his watch and sat up to fix her hair and make-up. He leaned against the sink and watched her. She hummed happily as she took her compact out of her purse and used it to apply more lipstick. He was glad that she wasn't upset by what happened.

He started to hum with her. Then he remembered some of the lyrics and started singing them: "*There may be trouble ahead, but while there's moonlight, and music and love and romance, let's face the music and dance...*" as he drunkenly waved his drink in time to the music. His date looked up from her compact and smiled when she saw that he knew the lyrics - not many though - they were quickly replaced by more humming. They both laughed. Now it was his turn to admire her. Despite her age, she was beautiful - blurred but beautiful. He tried to focus on her face, on her blonde hair and her dark red lips, as he continued to hum clumsily with her. Then he realised what they were doing. They were humming his mother's favourite song.

Still holding his drink, he asked what her name was again.

"I told you, my friends call me Blondine," she said coquettishly.

"No. Your real name," he demanded. "What's your real name?"

She seemed bothered by the question. "Why the sudden attitude?" she asked.

"What's your name?"

"Brooke. My name is Brooke. Why? Is there a problem?"

"Brooke from Ridgecrest?"

She looked up from her compact. "Do we know each other?" she asked guardedly.

"You were married to John Webster?"

"Well, yes, I was. But what's it to you?" she asked in a harder tone. "Did you know John?"

"I'm Blake Webster."

"Oh my god," she gasped.

Blake realised she was his mother. A thousand confusing thoughts went through his head. So many years had gone by and, suddenly, there she was in front of him. And they had just had sex. He was right when he had told Warren that she was probably a prostitute in Times Square. That's probably what she was. That's why she was at the Broadway.

He held his drunken head and sat down on the chair that she had been sitting on before, trying not to cry. He felt horrible. Guilty for having had sex with her. Angry because she had deserted him. But most of all, sad about all the years he had spent without her.

As if she was reading his mind, she got off the bed and put her arm around him in a supportive, motherly way. He had never felt such a gentle touch.

"I'm so sorry," she said. "For everything."

That did it. The tears came flooding down - from both of them.

His mother continued to explain, to apologise: "Blake, I love you. I love you as a son. It was horrible being with your father. I had to leave. He used to beat me. Blamed me for having a son. It got worse and worse. I was afraid I was going to kill him. I had to get out. He didn't need that stuff I took from the safe."

With tears streaming down his face, he said that it didn't matter. Nothing mattered. He was just happy to see her after all these years. He told her that he loved her, that he missed her, that he understood how she felt because he felt the same way. He had left too. Things had been great in New York at first but then he met Phil and started using drugs and things just started falling apart. He told her everything - about how he had killed José and how he was going away to find his grandmother. And how he had arranged for the murder of his own father, her husband.

She stood there, shocked. "Blake, look, don't worry, I'm on your side. I want to help. Where does the grandmother live?"

"You know," he said, "you're probably rich now. That donkey sanctuary he left his money to was a scam. It doesn't exist anymore."

"Blake, please let me help you. Where does the grandmother live?"

He didn't want to involve her in it. He told her she lived in Rome, that he was taking a flight from Newark to Rome early tomorrow and was going to try to find her. He figured he'd be back in a couple of weeks, if not sooner.

"But why? Why don't you stay here? I can help you."

"My flight's booked. Everything is arranged. I'm leaving in a few minutes. I'll be back. The room is booked until the end of January. We can talk about everything then. Here, take this..."

He handed her the note with the details of his father's lawyer that Warren had given him. He had already entered the lawyer's information in his phone.

"If you move from the hotel," he said, "tell Carlotta where you'll be." He took out a wad of bills from his pocket and tried to give her some.

"I don't need the money," she said. "Don't worry, I'll be here. You have no idea how much I missed you, all these years, my darling."

They traded phone numbers and he got his suitcase from the closet. He put on a coat that had his last bag of heroin in it. He would snort it in the cab. It wouldn't be the first time he had done drugs in a cab. That would be his last dose until he got to the Canaries where he could use Susan's methadone to detox.

"I'm sorry, I have to go," he said to his mother. He just wanted to get out of there now, to clear his thoughts, to make sure he didn't change his mind about the airport.

"Don't worry, I really will be back," he said and started to walk out the door. Then he turned around and went back to her, gave her a kiss on the cheek and hugged her good-bye.

"I'll be back!" he repeated as he ran out of the room.

Wiping away her tears, she listened to Blake walking down the hallway. When she couldn't hear his footsteps anymore, she waited five more minutes and then reached into her bag. Moving her small Smith & Wesson out of the way, she grabbed her phone and called her boss.

"Warren. You owe me for this, you really do... Yes, he believed me... Don't worry, I got a full confession."

She agreed to meet up at Gigi's. Warren was already there, finishing off his fourth cup of coffee. He had been waiting for her call.

21. The Getaway

Outside on the street, Blake flagged down the first available cab he could see through the fog of his tears and told the driver to get to JFK airport as quickly as possible. As they moved slowly through the Manhattan traffic, he slouched down in the back seat and snorted the small bag of heroin he had brought with him with a hundred-dollar bill. It was his last bag.

"Hey, what do you think you're doing?" the driver protested.

Blake gave the bill to the driver and told him to keep it.

"Gee, thanks buddy. You can do whatever you want in this cab."

Blake sat back and tried to figure out what had just happened in his hotel room. Every time he gathered his thoughts, the drink and drugs he had taken un-gathered them. How could that woman be his mother? It was just too much of a coincidence. But if she wasn't his mother, how could she have known his mother's name? And what about that song she had been humming? Or her blonde hair and dark red lipstick? The only person who knew that much about his mother was Lieutenant Warren.

Warren! That was the missing link. It all fell together. What a sap he had been. That woman must have been a cop. She and Warren and had planned the whole thing. "Blondine" had been moved into the room next door to make sure they would meet. He had fallen for their trap, hook line and sinker. They now had a full confession from him. He had confessed to a cop. Thank god, he hadn't told her where he was really going. It was now a race to get there.

He told himself to stay focused on his plan. He had to find José's grandmother and give her a share of the loot. She deserved a cut more than anyone else. What happened to him after that was up to the cops and the justice system. But the important thing was to find the grandmother. He prayed to a god that he no longer believed in that Warren and his cronies didn't find him first.

* * * * *

Blake was right about the blonde next door, of course. Her real name was Angela Williams - the same Angela Williams who had helped Lieutenant Warren out on the Gilman case. While Blake was rushing to the airport, she was talking to the lieutenant over a plate of Luigi's homemade lasagne:

"But you don't understand, Warren. I let him fuck me. That's entrapment."

"Who's gonna know?" Warren replied. "What jury is going to believe a junkie model over a hard-working female cop with impeccable credentials and backed up by her boss - me? But I doubt if it will ever get to court. I think I know Blake pretty well. He'll come clean once he's caught. He's a small-town boy, not a career criminal."

"You sound like you've got a soft spot for the kid."

"I do. He sort of reminds me of me before I joined the force. We had similar childhoods. His dad was scum and so was mine. But I had a cop friend who turned out to be a saviour."

"Maybe you could be Blake's saviour."

Warren laughed. "When his case comes up, I'll put in a good word. He'll probably end up accepting a plea bargain - maybe serve ten or fifteen-years max. He'll still have his whole life in front of him when he gets out. I wish I did."

"You're not that old, Harry. Your ticker might be old but you're not. I used to have the hots for you when I first joined the force. A lot of the women recruits did."

She changed the subject when he started to turn red. He didn't mention that he had been attracted to her as well. He didn't need to.

"Have you put a tracer out on Blake?" she asked.

"Yeah. I've got Customs working on it. All the airlines at Newark with flights going to Rome have received his passport details and a photograph. I'd be surprised if he isn't picked up in the next hour or so. They're going to call me."

Warren watched as Angela bent forward to scoop up another forkful of lasagne in her slinky, low cut, undercover dress. He couldn't help but feel a little excited. He wondered why they had never had sex. A lost opportunity. He would never have considered a relationship with a recruit back then. Now, he wasn't so sure. He still had feelings for her. She'd make a good wife.

"I felt horrible pretending to be his mother. It must be a total head-fuck for him. What happened to his real mother?"

"Who knows? She disappeared from the radar."

"Who gets the inheritance?"

"Blake does. Unless the real Mrs. Webster pops up."

"I'm surprised they never got a divorce."

"How could they? He didn't know where she was. As far as he was concerned, all of his money was going to a donkey sanctuary."

"A what?"

"It's a long story."

Lieutenant Warren's phone rang. It was the captain. The results from Newark had come back and Blake wasn't booked on any flights to Rome.

"And there's another thing," Seligman said. "Narcotics busted the Hole in The Wall. I knew it was happening but couldn't let anyone know, at least not anyone who wasn't directly involved in the operation."

"And?"

"One of the spotters they picked up said he had witnessed a death in the alleyway. Sounded like José's murder. He saw the whole thing. Phil was the one who was in charge. He got the dope, and he stuck the needle in the guy's arm. He tried to get Blake to do it, but Blake nodded off. When he woke up, Phil convinced him that he killed José. The spotter said he could hear their conversation - the sound bounced off the alley walls - there was an echo."

"Do you mean Blake is innocent?"

"That depends on who you believe. Maybe the spotter had an axe to grind with Phil. And what about Blake's confession to Angela? Why would he lie about his flight details to someone he considered to be his long-lost mother? Something is fishy. I'm getting Customs to check all airlines at both Newark and JFK for all destinations. Can you give Phil and Susan a visit?

"Sure, I'd be happy to. Listen, I'm with Angela right now. At Gigi's..."

"Don't let that Italian mobster hear any of this!"

The lieutenant looked around and saw Luigi wiping down the surface of the counter. He didn't look like he had heard anything.

"I'd be surprised if that old guy could hear anything from where he is," Warren told his boss.

He was wrong. Luigi had become an expert at listening in on other people's conversations over the years. His age hadn't affected his hearing, but he didn't mind being pigeon-holed into the category of "old man" by the cops. It made him appear more innocent than he was. Who would suspect an "old man" like him - an Italian Mr. Friendly who owned the corner diner - of having a storeroom full of cocaine?

"Do you mind if Angela comes along?" Warren asked Seligman. "Susan will be there - a female cop might come in handy." He looked at Angela who nodded enthusiastically. It didn't go unnoticed by Luigi who had already figured out she was an undercover officer.

"I don't mind if she doesn't mind. I'll consider it overtime," Seligman answered.

"Ok, thanks." Warren hung up his phone and looked at Angela.

"You're in," he said.

"Let's go," she responded. The lasagne can wait."

22. The Cop-Killer

As soon as Warren and Angela left the restaurant, Luigi borrowed one of the waiters' phones and rang Phil. He warned him that Warren and "some undercover broad" were on their way to his apartment to ask him about a murder.

"Look Phil, I don't know what you've been up to, and I don't want to know - I'm not involved. Whatever it is, blame it on Blake. They already have a confession from him. And don't let Susan talk to the cops."

"Blake confessed to both murders?"

"I told you, I'm not involved! I don't know anything about any murders! Except maybe the one that's going to happen when I wring your neck the next time that I see you. They were talking about José and Blake's father.

"What sort of confession?"

"I'm not sure. I couldn't hear everything. The undercover cop got it out of him."

"So why do they want to talk to me?"

"How should I know? I told you I'm not involved. This call never happened. Do you understand?"

"Okay, okay, already. I get it. Don't worry, I'm not going to involve you in anything."

"Do you still have that pistol I gave you?"

"Do you think I'll need it?" He was getting scared.

"No. But make sure you hide it somewhere. I don't want them finding it. You haven't pawned it, have you?"

"Of course not."

"I should have never given it to you. Anyway, it sounded like they don't have a warrant, so you don't even have to let them in. And don't do anything stupid."

"Okay Uncle Luigi. *Non problema!*"

He hated when Phil tried to speak Italian. He'd never even been to Italy. "*Idiota!* he shouted into the phone. And how many times do I have to tell you - stop fucking calling me uncle!

Luigi hung up. He knew he would have to tell his bosses about what was going on. He felt horrible, ratting on his own nephew, but what could he do? If he didn't report him, Luigi could get into trouble. He hoped they wouldn't see his nephew as an "expendable."

Phil wasn't too worried about the visit by Warren and his

colleague. He thought that the police would want to question him at some time or another. He was surprised they hadn't done it sooner. 'So, Blake had confessed,' he said to himself. That made things a lot easier. All he had to do was back up the confession, like his uncle said: "blame it on Blake."

Susan wasn't so cool. "What if you say something wrong?" she asked Phil. "What if they have a witness?"

He told her to shut up and stay in the bedroom while the cops were there. Let him do all the talking. She started to rant - "what if this happens and what if that happens..."

When she wouldn't shut up, he slugged her. She shut up. God, he was getting sick of her. He figured it would take at least fifteen minutes for the lieutenant and Miss Undercover to get there so he quickly took Susan into the bedroom so she could have a hit to calm down. As usual she couldn't find a vein and Phil had to shoot her up. She was fine after that. She sat on the bed peacefully scratching her nose. "Thanks darling. I love you," she said in baby goo-goo language. He noticed that a small bruise was forming under her eye where he hit her.

"Me too," he said. "And, just in case, here, take this." He reached under the bed and grabbed the small pistol his uncle had given him.

"What the fuck is this?" she screeched.

"It's called a gun. All you have to do is pull the trigger and shoot – like in a cowboy movie." He took the safety catch off and placed it in the drawer next to their bed - where Susan kept her works.

"Only use it if they try to shoot me," he said, "but don't worry, it won't come to that."

Susan's wide eyes eventually narrowed and then closed completely as she nodded off, mumbling "O.K."

Phil took out a larger gun - a semi-automatic Desert Eagle that he kept behind a small stack of clothes on the top shelf of their bedroom closet. His uncle didn't know about that gun. He had bought it from another dealer. He stuck it down the back of his jeans, making sure it was hidden under the loose black sweatshirt he was wearing. From his front pocket he took out a small wrap of crystal meth and rolled out a line on the table next to the bed. He had just started to snort it when there was a knock on the door.

"Answer it!" he shouted to Susan, "and then come straight back into the bedroom."

"But I thought you said not to talk to them."

"I did. But I have to finish this line. Just answer the fucking door and I'll come out." It wasn't just the line he was worried about. He didn't want to answer the door himself in case there were a load of cops there. If necessary, he could escape through the fire escape outside the bedroom window, while they arrested Susan.

"Don't say anything important," he told her before she left the bedroom. "They'll probably ask for me. Just yell out my name and I'll come out. Then you go into the bedroom, and I'll talk to them. But, whatever you do, don't let them in. If they say they have a warrant, ask to see it."

"A what?" she asked from dreamland.

"Just don't let them in!"

Susan was never very good at following directions. When she answered the door, she held it wide open like she would do for anyone who visited. Angela noticed the bruise on her face.

Warren asked if they could talk to Phil.

"Oh sure," Susan said, scratching her nose. "Phil!" she shouted.

Nothing happened.

"Phil!" she shouted again.

When he didn't answer the second time, she told the cops to "wait a second" and went into the bedroom to get him. He had just finished the line and was putting the wrap underneath the mattress when they heard the cops on the other side of the closed bedroom door.

"Is everything okay in there, Susan?" Angela asked, tapping the door with a few gentle knocks. Susan had left the front door open when she went to get Phil in the bedroom, allowing the cops to walk right in. They could always argue later that, because of the bruise, they thought she was in danger.

Susan opened the bedroom door slightly and peered out. She was surprised to see the cops in the apartment, but not as surprised as Phil.

"What the fuck! Do you have a warrant?" he shouted out from behind his girlfriend, his eyes bulging from the meth.

"Susan let us in," Warren said, pushing his way into the bedroom.

Angela asked Susan again if she was okay. She hated guys who beat up on women.

"Susan, if you're in trouble, I can take you someplace safe."

Warren looked around the bedroom for stolen goods. The bedroom was as messy as the living room. It didn't look like the apartment of newly made millionaires. Then he noticed an overstuffed suitcase and a Luis Vuitton bag. He'd love to have a look in those. But Phil was right. They didn't have a warrant. He had to be careful. He took a chance:

"Phil, what happened to all the stuff from the robbery in Ridgecrest?" he asked.

Susan had sat down on the bed but jumped back up when Warren asked his question. "What robbery in Ridgecrest?" she asked. "Never heard of the place." She sat down again, scratching her nose, again.

"I was talking to Phil," Warren said.

Angela's attention was on Susan. She wanted to get her away from Phil.

"Susan, do you need help? I'm here to help you. Why don't you come back to the precinct with me? I can find you a safe place to stay."

Susan stood up and began walking toward Angela like she was going to leave with her. That's all Phil needed. She knew everything and would probably let it all out at the first sign of kindness. Sometimes he hated girls. There was no way that he was going to let Susan go with the cop. Feeling indestructible from the meth he had snorted earlier, he pulled the gun out from the back of his jeans and pointed it at his girlfriend.

"Listen, you fucking bitch. You're not going anywhere. There's a limit to my kindness."

"Whoa, Phil, it was just a question. Calm down," Angela said. She had to be careful. He looked out of it. His pupils were dilated. "Drop the gun, Phil. Don't be stupid."

Warren took out his own gun and backed up a few steps, so his aim covered the whole room. Seeing the stoned confusion on Phil's face, he repeated Angela's command by shouting, in no uncertain terms, "DROP THE GUN PHIL!" He wanted Phil to know that he meant business.

Angela tried to diffuse the situation. She was afraid that Warren was going into hero mode. Why did men always have to act so macho?

"Warren, please, let me handle this." She turned back to Phil, "Nobody is going to get hurt Phil. When you put your gun away, Warren will put his away. Everything is cool."

"Handle *this* you bitch." Phil turned from Susan to Angela.

He shot her once in the chest and she fell to her knees, before hitting the floor. Susan got the pistol out of the drawer and pointed it at Warren so he wouldn't shoot Phil. Having taken care of Angela, Phil was pointing his gun at Susan again whose face was clouded with confusion. She didn't know who the enemy was anymore.

"You think we had anything to do with murdering José?" Phil shouted to Warren. "That was all Blake's doing. He hated José because of the competition. He lured him into the alleyway. Blake did the Ridgecrest job too. He killed his own father."

"Drop the fucking gun, Phil. NOW!" Warren shouted.

Phil pulled the trigger and Susan fell to the floor. Warren pulled his trigger and shot Phil more than enough times to kill him. He saw that Susan was still breathing so he went over to check on Angela. He tried to find her pulse. There wasn't one. He held his head to her chest but couldn't hear anything.

"Fuck!" he said. "Angela, I'm so sorry. This is my fault. I'm so sorry." He held on to her lifeless body, praying for a miracle. It never came. Instead, he heard Susan gurgling on the other side of the room. She was still alive.

"Kill the bastard," she mumbled, not realising that Phil was already dead. "He's a creep. Blake didn't kill José. He did. He told me after it happened. He came home all pleased with himself - he was bragging - 'another one bites the dust' - thought it was funny. Blake nodded off before he got to José."

Her breathing became increasingly laboured. She was trying to say something, but she could only get one word out: "Ridgecrest."

"Ridgecrest!" Warren repeated. "What happened in Ridgecrest, Susan? Tell me!"

"Blake's dad was already dead. Phil said that we had to make it seem like we killed him so that Blake would still share the money with us. He wanted to have control over Blake..."

"Where's Blake, Susan?" Warren shouted angrily through his tears. "Where the fuck is Blake?"

She didn't answer. She was dead.

23. Candy on the Beach

While forensics was surveying the murder scene at Phil's apartment in New York, Blake was arriving at Las Palmas airport. Getting through customs at JFK was easy. Nobody took any notice of the small bottle of 'aftershave' - Susan's methadone - that he had packed with his other toiletries; nor did they notice the cash, gold rings, bracelets, and watches that were distributed randomly among his clothes in his luggage.

At Las Palmas, the Spanish authorities waved everyone through without checking anything. They were more worried about interrupting the flow of the incoming tourists than they were in checking for contraband. Blake walked straight through customs without being checked. The airport lobby was on ground level so all he had do to was walk outside to get a cab. It had been winter in New York; in the Canaries, it was like summer. Although he couldn't see the ocean from outside the airport, Blake could certainly feel it. It felt like freedom.

He got into the cab at the front of a line of cabs and asked the driver to take him to the Yumbo Centre in clumsy Spanish that he had learned from the internet: "Yo voy a la Yumbo Centre, por favor."

"What did you say mate?" the cab driver asked.

"Are you English?" Blake asked, surprised.

"Everybody is English in the Canaries, mate. You sound like a Yank. Not many of them around."

Blake felt like hugging the guy for being so friendly.

"Yeah, I'm from California," he said, "but I've been living in New York."

"You're not with that new Bond movie, are you? They're supposed to be filming a Bond movie somewhere on the island. You look like a movie star. Have I seen you before?"

Blake laughed. At least he hadn't asked him if he was a model. "No, I'm not a movie star."

"Criminal?"

"Huh?"

"A lot of people who end up here are running away from one criminal activity or other - tax evaders, drug dealers, money launderers, that sort of thing. They'll take anybody's cash over here. They don't care how you got it."

"No, I'm not a criminal. I just needed some sunshine."

"Gay?" the driver asked.

"No, what gave you that idea?"

"The Yumbo is full of gay bars - at least at night. Not that I have anything against gay people," he was quick to stress. "There's probably more gay people than straight in this part of the Canaries. The gays and the criminals keep this place running. But you're neither of those are you?" he asked, as he checked out Blake's reaction in the rear-view mirror.

As a fan of gangster films, the cabbie was dying to meet one in real life. Although he 'knew' that there were gangsters in the Canaries, he had never actually met any and hoped that Blake might fit the bill. He was disappointed when his passenger didn't react to his 'criminal' comment but consoled himself with the thought that, maybe, that's exactly what a criminal would do – 'not react.'

"Are there any hotels in the Yumbo Center?" Blake asked.

"No, just bars and a sauna." he answered. "Different strokes for different folks. Leather bars for the S & M crowd, discos for the dancers and Ginger's bar where they do a drag show. Straight people go there too, just for the show. It's an institution. Been there loads of times with my mates. There it is up there," the driver motioned with his head. "The Yumbo."

It didn't look like it was filled with nightclubs. It looked like an outdoor mall of tacky souvenir shops. As they got closer, they passed quite a few hotels and apartment complexes with vacancy signs. One complex stood out; a small run-down building with large neon letters stuck to its roof announcing "El Nirvana." Someone had forgotten to turn off the neon in the daylight and the letters flashed intermittently, like they didn't know if it was day or night.

"Could you stop here?" Blake asked the cab driver.

"Here? Are you sure?"

"Yeah, why?"

"The locals call it the crack hotel." the driver explained. "There are all sorts of weirdos living there. It doesn't even have a swimming pool."

"That's okay. I'll be spending most of my time on the beach. It looks cheap."

"Oh yes, it's cheap alright."

The driver stopped the cab in front of the reception office and started to help his customer with his bags. Blake insisted that he could take care of them.

"Are you sure? They're pretty heavy. What do you have in there, a dead body?" he joked. Blake didn't laugh. 'Maybe he really is a gangster,' the cabbie thought.

"How much do I owe you?" Blake asked.

"30 dollars. Standard rate from the airport."

Blake gave him fifty.

"Thanks. I can tell you're not English. They never tip. Here, take my card. Might come in handy someday."

Blake took the card and lugged his two heavy suitcases through the glass doors of the "Recepcion." A frail-looking woman with black frizzy hair greeted him from behind a peeling, laminated counter.

"Buenos Dias" she said, with a mostly toothless grin. Then in English: "What can I do for you?"

"You speak English?" Blake asked.

"Of course. Everyone here does. *¿Qué quieres?*"

Despite her frailty, she spoke with the directness of someone much younger; someone you wouldn't want to mess with.

"Do you have a room for rent?"

"A room? Nobody rents a room in the Playa del Ingles. They rent apartments. *Apartamentos*," she stressed. "I can give you our luxury suite for $500 a week. How about that?"

Blake was sure she was overcharging him but thought her dishonesty might come in handy later, in case anyone came looking for him. He agreed to take the apartment, sight unseen. She opened a guestbook on the top of the counter and Blake noticed there were track marks on her paper-thin arms. He signed in with fake name. When she asked for his passport, he fumbled in his pockets and produced his wallet instead. She could see it was full of cash.

"I'm sorry I must have put it into one of my bags – can I give it to you later?" He handed her $500 in cash for the apartment.

"Gracias," she said, smiling. "And a twenty-dollar processing charge," she added, holding out her palm. He paid it without asking any questions.

"C'mon *guapo*, I'll show you to your apartment," she said as she grabbed one of his bags. "So heavy."

"Don't worry, I can carry it." He quickly took it from her.

"Do I still get my tip?" she asked, joking.

"I just gave you $20."

"That was an application fee."

He gave her another twenty.

"Don't worry about finding that passport," she said, as she walked back to the desk.

"*Gracias,*" Blake responded.

"*De nada.*"

* * * * *

It was fairly crowded by the time Blake got to the beach. Before he did anything else, he wanted to get some colour on his face to fit in with the rest of the tourists. Sunbathing would also give him time to come up with a plan for finding José's grandmother. He had been so focussed on getting to the Canaries that he had no idea of how he was actually going to find the grandmother now that he was there. He remembered that José said her name was Luisa and wondered how many people named Luisa Fernandez lived in the area.

He rented a sun lounger and dragged it to a section of the beach that was devoid of tourists, a small area of rocky sand near a disused jetty. He closed his eyes and listened to the waves gently lapping the shore, one after another, like a peaceful chant. 'Maybe Phil wasn't such a bad guy after all,' he thought. 'Maybe things really will be alright after all,' he reassured himself, not knowing that his friend's body was already in the morgue.

Blake was on the verge of dozing off when a dark shadow suddenly appeared above him, blocking out the sunlight. He assumed it was a cloud that would soon float away but it stayed where it was, weaving back and forth. He opened his eyes and saw a curvy blonde looking down at him, holding an open bottle of Cava.

'Another blonde,' he thought, remembering his neighbour – the cop who had pretended to be his mother. But this blonde was different. She was younger, closer to his age, and her hair was platinum like Marilyn Monroe's. She was even dressed like a showgirl in a tight, flesh-coloured outfit, studded with gold sequins, that clung to every curve. A small moon-shaped purse hung from her shoulder.

"Hi. I'm Candy," she said when he opened his eyes.

"Hi."

"Do you mind if I sit down?" she asked in an English accent, before falling onto the lounger. Blake moved over to give her some space. She took a swig from the bottle and handed it to him.

"Last night's club seems to last longer and longer," she said to nobody in particular as she stared out at the sea.

Blake took a drink from the bottle and handed it back. She took another swig and asked, "Do you think it ever ends, or does it just go on forever and ever?

"What?"

"The sea."

"Have you been up all night?" Blake asked.

"Night, day, whatever..." she answered with a flourish of her hand. "Would you like a fag?"

"Excuse me?"

"Oh, sorry, you're a Yank. Cigarette. Would you like a cigarette?"

"Yeah, sure."

She took a scrunched-up pack of red Marlboros from her purse, handed him one, and took the last one for herself. She tried to light his with a cheap, souvenir lighter, but couldn't quite hit her target.

"Here, let me help you." Blake wrapped his hand loosely around her wrist and guided it first to her cigarette, and then to his.

"Thank you," she said as some of her ash hit his chest. He quickly wiped it off.

"You're welcome."

They sat and watched the sea in silence, passing the bottle between them.

"It's like staring out at eternity," she said.

"Where were you last night? At a club? He asked.

"Ginger's."

"Ginger's at the Yumbo Centre?"

"Oh, do you know it?"

"I've heard of it, but I've never been there."

"I do a show there. Sometimes I have a drink after the show."

Quite a few drinks he imagined.

"Isn't it a gay club?" he asked.

"Gay, straight, whatever," she said with another flourish of her hand.

"Do women sing there?"

She laughed. "Yes, they most certainly do. I'm a woman." She squinted to get a better look at him. She liked what she saw.

"Are you gay or straight?"

"Straight."

She seemed surprised. She sat up as if she was trying to be on her best behaviour and then slumped back down, again. "Yeah, sure you are."

He laughed. "I am! 100 percent."

"I'll drink to that," she said as she slugged down the Cava.

"You didn't happen to know a guy called José at the Yumbo Centre, did you?" Blake asked.

"That would be like me going to New York and asking if you knew someone named Joe. It's a pretty common name here."

"His last name was Fernandez. He was living with his grandmother here, before he moved to New York."

"I'd love to go to New York," she said wistfully.

"I used to feel like that."

"What happened?"

"Nothing. Nothing happened."

She wondered what his story was, why he was on his own. Straight guys were a rarity on that part of the island.

"Are you a cop?" she asked.

"No, I'm not a cop," he answered.

"I like you. You seem nice." She reached into her purse and gave him a flyer for Ginger's.

"Here. Take this. Come and see the show tonight."

"Okay, but tell me, did you know José?"

"Sure. Everyone knew José. Come to the show and we'll talk."

She caressed his cheek several times, like she was petting a cat, and then tried to stand up. It took a few attempts, but she finally made it.

"Come to the show," she repeated before she left. He watched her walk away, her hips swaying side to side as she walked through the sand, trying not to fall over in her heels. He looked forward to visiting Ginger's that night.

24. Ginger's

As soon as Blake got to Ginger's, he wanted to leave. Candy's flyer said it opened at 7 pm but it was now 8 pm and hardly anybody was there. The Yumbo Centre was a strange place. Rather than being the nightclub mecca he had imagined, it was almost empty. Most of the bars were closed and he couldn't tell if they were permanently closed or just hadn't opened yet.

Ginger's was on the second floor. A thick velour curtain hid the stage at the back. In front of it was a series of small white plastic tables that extended onto the public walkway. The only customers were Blake and a few men nursing an assortment of cocktails in a multitude of colours. 'How many umbrellas, cherries on toothpicks and palm trees could you fit in one drink?' he wondered.

Blake saw someone peeking out from the stage curtain who eventually came out to take his order. He must have been a performer working as a waiter when the show wasn't on; he seemed to be in some type of costume. Even though he was a man he was dressed in a pair of hot pants, like a woman would wear – but he was definitely a man, judging from the bulge in the crotch of his shorts that was surrounded by rhinestones. He was wearing false eyelashes and lots of mascara but had a short military-style cropped haircut.

"What can I get you, babes?" he asked. "A cocktail? (pause) or just a cock?" he asked, as though he expected a "de-dum" from a (non-existent) house drummer.

Blake laughed. "Are you from England?" he asked.

"Yeah, babes. Essex. Do you know it?"

"Um, no, I've never been to England."

"A Yank, eh? What can I get ya?"

"I guess I'll have a cocktail. Is whiskey a cocktail?"

"It'll do."

"And do you do burgers or anything like that? I'm starving."

"Sure do," the waiter answered in a not very good American accent.

"Great. I'll have a cheeseburger and fries."

"No problema, babes."

He disappeared behind the stage curtain to get the drink. The bar in the main room wasn't open yet. He came back with two drinks – a whiskey and a shot of tequila. As he put the shot down, he said, "this is from Candy."

'So, she knows I'm here,' Blake thought.

Everyone in the show knew he was there. The waiter had made a fuss about "the gorgeous American" out front when he went to the backstage to get his whiskey. Candy had peeked out from the curtain and saw it was *her* American.

"Tell her thanks." He said to the waiter before holding up the shot to the curtain and downing it in one, in case Candy was watching. He handed the empty shot glass to the waiter.

"Are you sure you've never been to Essex?" the waiter asked.

Blake laughed and started on the whiskey.

"Oh, don't forget about the burger and fries,"

The waiter snapped his fingers.

"Oh yeah, food," he said. "I almost forgot what it was." Then he went to the burger stand next door and ordered a hamburger and fries, forgetting to tell them to put cheese on the burger.

As Blake nursed his whiskey, more people showed up – all very merry, probably had been drinking beforehand. He figured that the other bars must be opening. When his food arrived, he ordered another whiskey. The waiter curtsied this time and went to the bar in the main room, which was open now. After that drink arrived, the show began.

A gruff voice announced over the loudspeaker, "Welcome to Ginger's. The best show at the Yumbo! Well, the only show at the Yumbo…"

The audience applauded and yelped as if on cue; like they had been here before.

The voice continued: "And now here's the girl you are all dying to hear, Miss Candy Dahl."

Blake noticed the announcer had referred to as "Miss." A good sign. At least she wasn't married.

The curtains parted and there was the drunken blonde that Blake had met on the beach. She was wearing another form-fitting dress – a white one this time. When the lights hit it in a certain way it was almost transparent. She started singing an old song that Blake recognised from one of his mother's records. He wasn't sure who sang it on the recording, but it was about someone named Candy. "*Candy, sweet, Candy....*" the lyrics went.

He loved her for singing it. It was like she was singing it directly to him. Afterwards, he ordered another drink. The drinks were even stronger there than they were in New York. He loved the show. He loved everything. He didn't recognise all the songs, but they were the types of songs his mother sang at home while she was doing the housework. Someday, he would find her, he was convinced of it, and it would be his real mother this time.

By the end of Candy's act, the audience was going crazy, and Blake was smashed. He couldn't remember how many whiskies he had drunk. He joined in on the standing ovation that Candy got from the crowd as she blew them kiss after kiss. He felt that she had aimed at least one at him, and he blew one back. When she finally left the stage, she gestured for him to follow. He asked for his bill, but by the time it came, another act had started, and he didn't want to interrupt it by going backstage. The new performer was a man in drag who had the same gravelly voice as the announcer. Blake realised that it was the *same* person. Someone from the audience yelled out "Ginger!"

'So that's Ginger,' Blake thought. Her cheap multi-coloured wig - the sort of thing a man would wear at a bachelor's party - accentuated her manly features. She looked like a truck driver. Blake was confused. If Ginger was a drag queen, what about Candy? She must be a man in drag as well. He felt, that once again, he had been taken for a ride. He was beginning to wonder if there were any honest people left in the world. What a fool he had been. He turned to leave the club.

Candy must have been peering out of the side curtain. As soon as he started to leave, she came out from behind the curtain and started to run after him.

"Blake, wait!" she yelled. The crowd loved the drama and started shouting things like "you go girl, or "don't let that man get away!" Blake thought he even heard someone ask, "he looks like the Style Raven guy."

Ginger joked about what was happening, yelling to Candy "Get back in your cage, girl. It's Mama's turn now!" The music started and her first song began: "Ready or not, here comes Mama, Mama's talkin' loud, Mama's doin' fine, Mama's gettin' hot, Mama's goin' strong..."

Blake recognised it as a song from an old musical he watched on television with his mother when he was a kid. "Gypsy." A musical about the stripper Gypsy Rose Lee. Candy had sung her song with her natural voice. Ginger was miming to a movie soundtrack.

Candy caught up with Blake outside.

"Please wait, Blake, *please*! Let me explain!" She grabbed his arm and said "We've got to talk. Let's go for a walk."

She led him down the boardwalk, past the tourists, until she found a quiet spot, facing the sea.

"This is my favourite spot. Nobody comes down here. There aren't any shops."

He looked at her under the moonlight. She looked so beautiful in her white dress. But was she a "she?"

"Okay," she said. "First, you should know I am a girl. A real girl. I was born a boy, but I never felt comfortable as one. I had the hormones of a girl. I had the full operation when I was sixteen and I've been a girl ever since. Yes, I perform at Ginger's and yes, it's a gay club, but I am 100% female. As much a female as you are a male."

"I, I don't know what to say," he stammered. "We, I, well, where I was brought up..." His voice trailed off. He didn't want to offend her. God, she looked beautiful in that dress. "It's, it's just that we didn't have people like you in Crumville."

"What the fuck is Crumville?" she asked.

"It's where I grew up."

"You didn't have women in Crumville?"

He didn't know what to say. After a few seconds of silence, they both started laughing. It was all so absurd. He didn't have to be told she was 100% female; he could see with his own eyes. Looking at her in that white dress, he couldn't help but be turned on.

"You know," he said, "underneath this moonlight you look like the most beautiful thing I've ever seen."

He put his arm around her tiny waist and kissed her on the lips. She wondered whether it was just a token kiss – to show that he wasn't prejudiced against 'people like her.' She had had so many bad experiences in the past. The men who were interested her in tended to be gangsters and criminals who wanted to see what it was like to have sex with a sex-change. But Blake seemed different to them. Or maybe she was so starved of affection that she fell in love with anyone who showed her a degree of kindness. All she wanted was a normal life, whatever that was.

He kissed her again. She returned the kiss. It had been a long time since a man had made her feel so light-headed. Then they stood together silently in the shadows, his arm around her waist and her head on his chest, listening to the muffled sounds of families playing games like "Spin the Wheel" further down the boardwalk. Everyone seemed to be having so much fun.

She had to be careful. She didn't want to get hurt again. She had told him a lot about her, but he had hardly told her anything about him. For all she knew, he could be just another criminal on the run in the Canaries.

"Now you know my story, so what's yours? Why are you in the Canaries, Blake?"

He didn't know what to say. How do you tell somebody you're a murderer?

When he didn't answer, Candy let him know that whatever it was, she was on his side. If he needed help, she might be able to arrange it.

"Blake, I sense you need a friend," she said, lighting another cigarette. "I know what that feels like. I needed a friend once. Maybe I still do. Take your time. You can trust me."

He looked at the sea. It was so dark and endless and foreboding. He began his confession. He told her everything, from the childhood beatings to making it in New York, to the murders of José and his father. When he finished, he turned to see her reaction, fearing what it would be.

"Hmmm." She said. "Style Raven. I thought I recognised you."

"Is that all you can say?"

She shrugged her shoulders and leaned her back on the boardwalk rail. "Nothing really surprises me anymore."

"You seem disappointed."

"I guess every girl wants a man with a house in the country and a white picket fence, but it rarely ends up that way."

"I don't know what to do," he said. "I've got to find José's grandmother before the cops find me."

"José was a friend, Blake. He used to come to Ginger's after work. Most of the barmen do. She sells them coke, or whatever else they want. During the day, this place is a mecca for families hunting down souvenirs. At night, the clubs open, and the partying begins and doesn't stop. It just moves to a different location. Usually the dunes."

"Do you know where his grandmother lives?"

"It shouldn't be difficult to find out. Ginger should be able to help you out with that. She's kind of like a fairy godmother. She helps people out with a lot of things. She'll get you a new passport if you want one, under a different name, for a price of course. Where are you staying?"

"At El Nirvana."

"That dump? That'll be the first thing we'll change."

"You're talking like a criminal."

"I *am* a criminal, Blake. Why do you think I'm living in the Canaries? Do you need anything else?"

"Well, there's one other thing I should tell you about."

"There always is."

"I'm addicted to heroin. I've got enough methadone to last a few days, but I'm going to need some smack."

"It's never easy, is it," she said, mostly to herself. "Don't worry, Ginger can take care of it. She's been running the drugs market in this part of the Canaries for years. The cops know, but they also know that the tourists need their drugs. It's one of the things that bring them here. Otherwise, they'd all end up in Ibiza. We'll talk to Ginger after the next show. I've got to go now, it's almost showtime."

As they approached the club, he mustered up the courage to ask another question: "Candy, is Ginger a man or a woman?"

"When I first met her, she definitely still had a cock."

"How did you know?"

"I saw it when she was getting dressed backstage. But that was a long time ago. Now, nobody knows. Her five o'clock shadow suggests "man," but she insists that she's had the full operation. Most people think she still has a cock. A lot of straight men like to be fucked up the ass by a woman."

25. A New Identity

When Blake woke up the next afternoon, he was living somewhere else. He had moved his stuff from El Nirvana to a gated apartment complex owned by Ginger. After last night's show, Candy and Blake had a conversation with Ginger who agreed to help Blake out. The first thing she did was arrange for him to move to an apartment in her compound. Candy lived in a different apartment in the same group of apartments. Ginger's house was outside the gated complex, but not far. She lived in a large mansion in a residential area of the Playa del Ingles that few tourists saw. Her place was huge, with two swimming pools and too many bedrooms to remember. Her cleaning staff would probably know. The road to the property was hidden behind dense foliage and protected by two security gates with a guard at the front door.

Ginger jokingly referred to the compound that Candy and Blake lived in as "The Hellhole," even though it was anything but. Blake's apartment was even more luxurious than the place he had when he was working for Slick. All the rooms had marble floors. The bathroom even had marble walls. The living room was carpeted with Turkish rugs and cushions, and plush modular furniture that could easily be configured to meet any social need, particularly an all-night party. It would be a perfect space to lay around with a group of friends and get stoned.

The compound was almost as secure as Ginger's mansion. The floor to ceiling windows of the apartments were protected by metal gates and there was a complicated buzzer system to let visitors in. Blake had woken up to the sound of a buzzer but wasn't sure what he was supposed to do about it. Eventually the noise stopped, but then there was another buzzer and finally someone knocking loudly on the front door. He got up and answered it naked, expecting to see Candy. They had spent the night together but she wasn't in bed when he woke up. He didn't remember her leaving, but both of them had got pretty stoned on an assortment of drugs that Ginger had supplied in exchange for a small gold bracelet that Blake had dug out of his luggage. The bracelet was too small for her chunky wrist, but she said she could get it fixed. She didn't give them any heroin but almost everything else – lots of cocaine, rohypnol and a large bag a marijuana. She also threw in a magnum of Cava from behind the stage bar. He didn't know what to think about Ginger. It was nice of her to give them all that stuff but there was something about her that he didn't trust.

Bleary-eyed, Blake pursed his lips, preparing to give Candy a kiss, and opened the front door. Instead of Candy, Ginger walked in like a storm trooper with two of her cronies. He unpursed his lips and rushed into the bedroom to put on a pair of jeans and t-shirt. Ginger looked around the living room - at the overflowing ashtrays, the rizla packages on the floor, the Cava stains on her precious rugs, and the random socks and underwear that were strewn about.

"No pizza boxes?" she asked sarcastically. They actually did have a pizza but left the empty box in the kitchen.

"Well, I certainly hope you had a good time," she added.

"Don't worry, I'll clean up the mess," Blake said immediately.

"Blake, I assume Candy went over the security arrangements here with you? It's very important."

"Yes, she did, but I, um..." He had no idea what she was talking about. The rohypnol had erased most of his memory.

"O.K. Blake. Please. Pay Attention. Atención!" She clapped her hands twice quickly, to snap him to attention and started explaining the security system:

"There is a small screen built into the table next to the bed. There's another one over there." She pointed to a side table next to one of the modular chairs. "When you hear the buzzer, look at the screen and see who is trying to come through the main gates. They have to type in a code for your apartment. That code changes every day and will be sent to you each morning on your phone. Look at the screen and if you know who the visitor is, press the red button to open the main gates. The green button unlocks your front door. There's four locks on your front door that can only be opened from the outside if you know the code which is different than the code for the main gates. You don't need a code to lock or unlock your apartment from the inside, you just have to press the small buttons on the deadbolts – there are four of them – green, red, orange and grey - one for each lock. Is that clear? The reason I had to resort to knocking was because the security arrangements were not followed. I don't like to knock, Blake. It hurts my knuckles. Do you understand? The last thing we need are strangers snooping around."

"Yeah, sure," he said, not taking any of it in. Candy could

explain it all later.

"If you ever can't get into your apartment, call me. I know all the codes and have keys to everything. Now, let me introduce my friends – that's my driver Lucca – "Lucky Lucca," he is sometimes called and that's my bodyguard "Manuel" who is often referred to as 'Rider.'"

Lucca was dressed in a dark suit, his thick black hair greased back with gel, his skin so pale that he looked like he had never seen the sun in the sunniest place on earth. "Rider" was the complete opposite. With his long brown hair and flip flops, he looked like Jim Morrison of The Doors – some of the druggier cafes in town still played their music. His nickname, "Rider," was a reference to The Doors' song "Riders on the Storm."

Having introduced her "assistants," Ginger held out her hand in Manuel's direction and shouted, "Rider! *Pasaporte!*" He took a passport out of the back pocket of his ripped-up jeans and gave it to his boss who threw it on a glass coffee table in front of Blake who picked it up and opened it. His picture was the same, but his name had been changed to Miles Fenwick and a new date of birth added.

Ginger then asked Manuel for the "stuff," again holding out her hand. He pulled out a plastic bag of glassine envelopes from his pocket, each stamped "Kinky."

"Here's the dope I promised you last night," she said as she threw the bag onto the coffee table with a pack of disposable syringes.

"Being stoned isn't against the law here; neither is possession of a small amount for personal use. Just don't take more than one bag out with you. Otherwise, you could be done for dealing."

"I probably won't even need that much," Blake said. "I'm using it to withdraw."

"Whatever."

"Ginger, why are you doing all this for me?"

"We take care of our friends in the Canaries," she said. "We're *muy sympatico* here, aren't we Rider?

Rider agreed enthusiastically: "*Si, muy sympatico.*"

"I appreciate it," Blake said, looking at the dope on the table. He couldn't wait to try it.

"Do you want some money? he asked. "There must be something I can do for you in return."

Ginger stared at his crotch and laughed. "Oh, I can think of quite a few things, *guapo*."

He shifted embarrassedly.

"Don't worry," she said. "I know you're Candy's. But yes, there is something. I need you to take a holiday. Nothing major. Just a short holiday. A few days away. It will do you good."

"What do you mean?"

"Have you ever been to London, Blake?"

"No. Why London?

"You'll love London. It's like America, only older."

"What's the catch?"

"No catch. Candy said you had a lot on your mind so we thought it would be nice if you took a break."

"I'm already on a holiday."

"No, you're not. You're on a getaway."

"And when am I supposed to go on this holiday?"

"We have to sort some things out first. Sunday would be a good time to leave. We'll need you to pick up some money while you're there - the backers of the club like to pay in cash."

"I see. So, you want me to pick up some money for you. I don't feel comfortable with that."

Ginger picked up the dope and the syringes. "I'm sorry to hear that."

"Wait a second. I didn't say I wouldn't do it. You're right. I could use a break."

She put the stuff back on the table.

"Don't worry about packing," she told him. We'll give you a couple of suitcases to take with you."

He got the message. There was nothing *sympatico* about Ginger or the rest of them. He thought about asking what would be in the suitcases but figured it would be better if he didn't know. Besides, she would only lie. Even if she told him the contents it was doubtful that she would tell him about the false bottoms or any of the other hiding places. All he wanted right now was to get a needle in his arm.

"Can Candy come with me on this trip?" he asked.

"No. You'll have to go alone, darling." When Ginger saw the look of disappointment on his face, she added, "Candy's next door turning a trick. I'll tell her you want to see her when she's finished."

So that was it. Candy was a prostitute. She hadn't mentioned that last night when she was pouring her heart out to him. She wasn't any better than Ginger or the rest of them. But was he?

At least Candy didn't go around murdering people.

"I'll go through the details of the trip with you after tonight's show," Ginger said. She felt happier now that she had burst the bubble of at least one of the lovebirds. She turned to Manuel and Lucca. "*Vamos*!" she commanded. They started to leave but stopped at the front door.

"I almost forgot this," Ginger said as she came back into the room and laid a small pistol on the table "It only takes 10 rounds, but I doubt if you'll need anything deadlier than that. It's just in case of an emergency. It's loaded. Put it someplace safe. If you need more rounds, let me know."

"But I don't even know how to use it."

"It's easy. It's a Glock 26. The important thing to remember is that it only has a two finger grip - Candy can show you how to use it."

Blake thought it was highly unlikely that he would ever need a gun. He left it on the coffee table. Ginger, Lucca and Rider jumped into Ginger's Range Rover. Although Lucca was officially the driver, Ginger usually preferred to drive. It made her feel superior to the small cars on the road which they treated like travelling ashtrays as they flicked their ashes at them, laughing whenever some of the ash flew through the open window of a family's station wagon and hit some of the passengers.

Ginger hated families, except for her own, of course, which largely consisted of Lucca and Manuel. They had been loyal to their boss for more than a decade and she had rewarded them generously over the years – both in drugs and cash. Candy had come into the picture later. She was like a stray dog they had rescued from an abusive owner so that they could abuse her themselves.

As soon as they were gone, Blake took the dope into the bedroom and treated himself to a substantial hit. He would start his detox tomorrow - "*mañana*." The Spanish stuff was brown, not white like in New York. He'd never had brown before. As soon as he injected it, he nodded off on the bed. It was pretty strong. When he opened his eyes, it was an hour later and Candy was standing at the bedroom door, watching him.

"I wondered where you went," he said. "You weren't here when I woke up this morning."

She looked different than last night. Her hair was tied back, and she was wearing a t-shirt with a palm tree on it and the words "Playa del Ingles." She looked like a tourist. He sat up and asked her how she got in.

"Even with all the security in this place, you're still supposed to lock the door, silly." She sat on the bed. He moved away from her.

"Candy, I've got some questions I need to ask you."

"I don't have much time. I've got a date with a bus stop."

"Huh?"

"Once a week, I sit on the bench at a bus stop like a tourist, with a large shopping bag from one of the souvenir shops in the Yumbo. Inside the bag is a load of cash. Two other tourists sit down next to me with a suitcase, like they're waiting for the shuttle to the airport. They stand up to light their cigarettes, and then keep on walking. One of them has the bag I was carrying. The shuttle arrives. When it leaves, I'm walking with the other tourists, the real tourists on the way to their hotels. I take my suitcase to Ginger's office, backstage at the club, and leave it there. The rest of my day is free."

"What's in the suitcase?"

"Some of the purest cocaine you'll ever taste, this side of the Rockies," she said in an American accent that made them both laugh.

"What happens to it?" Blake asked.

"Ginger arrives later in the afternoon with Lucca and Manuel. They cut the coke and divide it into small wraps which they distribute to the bars in the Yumbo. I get paid later that night by Ginger when I arrive to do my show."

"Isn't it dangerous?"

"Not really. I've been doing it so long that it's pretty boring. Anyway, it means I have the whole afternoon free after I've made the drop. What about meeting up later on the beach – the spot where I first met you? I can pick up a bottle of Cava on the way. We'll have a toast to the new you. I guess I'll have to start calling you Miles from now on."

"Candy, there's one thing I have to ask you, and I'd like to know the truth."

"What's that?"

"Ginger said you were turning a trick next door. Were you?"

She sat down on the bed. "Blake, look, I don't enjoy doing it but, it's unavoidable. I owe Ginger. She helped me out, like she's helping you out. She saved me from one gang so I could work for hers. Hers is better. They don't beat you up."

She paused and looked downward, avoiding Blake's glance. "I'm not a human anymore Blake, I'm a commodity."

"I'm sorry," he said, holding her hand like a schoolboy. "Don't worry, I'm not going to judge you. Who am I to judge?"

She shrugged her shoulders. "It's not a big deal. Everyone's a commodity in one way or another. Everything is so 'buy and sell' nowadays. So, I sell. I sell myself. When you came along, I thought that maybe, just maybe, you would be my way out. You seemed like the kindest person in the world. You still do"

"Listen Candy, why don't we just leave today? We can get a flight to New York tonight and start all over. The cops probably don't even suspect me. Phil's not the type to blab. It was a stupid idea to try and find José's grandmother. I've got a lot of money, Candy. We could get that house in the country with a picket fence that you've always dreamed of."

"There's one thing you're forgetting, Blake. You're a criminal, just like me and Ginger and practically everyone else in this god-forsaken place. You killed a model and you paid someone to kill your father. It's not so easy to escape from the criminal world once you've entered into it. We're stuck in a trap, Blake. We always will be. The people in control, people like Ginger, love living the way they do, but we're the ones that ultimately take the rap. We'll never get that picket fence Blake. It's somewhere over a rainbow that doesn't exist."

Candy was right, of course. They hadn't escaped from their pasts; they had merely traded one form of criminality for another. Blake wondered if they would ever be truly free or whether life was merely a series of repetitions that eventually led to death. He decided that the most honourable thing to do was to stick to his original plan of finding José's grandmother. He might not be able to escape his past, but he could, at least, make *her* future a little easier. He didn't know what would happen after that and he didn't care as long as he could spend another night with Candy. Even with everything that had gone on, he felt blessed to have found someone like her, his first real girlfriend. He told her that he would see her on the beach later, in the same spot where they had originally met. She gave him a double "thumbs up" and kissed him goodbye. He didn't know it at the time, but it would be their last kiss. He would never see her again.

26. Warren Gets Lucky

While Blake was lying on the beach waiting for Candy, Lieutenant Warren was stepping off a plane at Las Palmas airport. It hadn't taken long for the force to find out Blake's flight details, but he seemed to have disappeared once he got to Las Palmas. Hotels were supposed to take down the passport details of their guests but there was no trace of Blake after he got off the plane.

Before leaving New York, Warren had met with his Captain to go over the case. After what Susan had told him, he was convinced that Blake was innocent. Seligman wasn't so sure.

"Of course, she'd say that Blake was innocent, just to get back at Phil who had just shot her. She thought he was still alive. If Blake was innocent, why the quick getaway?" Seligman had asked.

He was right, of course. Except that Warren still thought Blake was innocent. He didn't seem capable of murder. But it was just a hunch, and you couldn't base an investigation on a hunch, as Seligman reminded him time and time again. You needed facts and the facts were that Blake had first confessed and then left the country. Not only had he left the country, he had also lied to a woman he thought was his mother about where he was going. He was as good at lying as any other criminal.

"Warren, a cop is dead. It's serious, now," Seligman had reminded him. "It's not just about a junkie model or a dead farmer anymore. You need to find Blake. We need to get him back here before his case gets tied up in a Spanish extradition court. You don't have the legal right to arrest him in Spain, but he won't know that. You need to get him to come back voluntarily if you can. It's all on your shoulders now. If you pull this off, you'll be back at the top of the game again. No forced retirement. An advancement maybe, but no forced retirement. I'll even give you an assistant for the physical stuff if you want."

Seligman's words – "no forced retirement" - were still going through Warren's head when he stepped out of the airport and into the bright sunlight of Las Palmas, feeling completely out of place in his grey New York raincoat. Whereas the sunshine had felt like freedom to Blake, it felt like 'sweat' to Warren. He got into the first cab in the long line of cabs outside and asked the driver to take him to the nearest five-star hotel to the Yumbo

Centre. Ava had mentioned that José had been "discovered" there. A "hunch" told him that Blake would probably end up there too. Otherwise, why would he fly to the Canaries?

"There aren't any five-star hotels at the Yumbo Centre," the cabbie said.

"Well, as close as you can get, then."

As the cab was making its way out of the airport, the driver looked into his rear-view mirror and asked his passenger if he was "here for the new Bond movie?"

"What new Bond movie?" Warren asked.

"They're supposed to be filming a new Bond movie here, but nobody knows where. I just thought with your raincoat and everything that you might be in it."

Seligman rolled his eyes and hoped that this driver wasn't going to talk all the way to the Yumbo.

"I picked up a guy a couple of days ago who looked just like Bond. He said he wasn't, but I bet he was. He had black hair and blue eyes, just like the original Bond."

Warren perked up. "Did you say black hair and blue eyes?"

"Yeah, except then he wanted me to drop him off at that crack hotel and I doubt if someone playing Bond would want to stay there."

"Listen. If I paid you, say $500, would you be my driver for the day? I've got a few places I need to check out."

"Yeah. Sure."

"Ok. Forget about the five-star hotel for the moment. Take me to the crack hotel."

"You want to go *there*?" The cabbie wondered why El Nirvana had suddenly become so popular.

"Just for a visit."

It wasn't as coincidental as it might seem that Warren got the same cab driver as Blake. Warren had taken the same flight as Blake, hoping that a staff member might remember him. One cabin steward thought he recognised him and was at least able to confirm that Blake was traveling by himself.

The cabbie always had luck with that particular flight. Most of the passengers on other flights took the shuttle into the Playa del Ingles, but there were usually quite a few passengers on that Air Morocco flight who travelled in cabs - businessmen in suits, usually from the Mideast, who gave big tips. He always made sure he was first in line for that flight, even if it meant giving passengers to other cabs.

He took Warren to El Nirvana, as requested. Inside the reception office the Lieutenant was greeted by the same toothless crack addict who had checked Blake in. Warren flashed his badge and showed her Blake's picture. She said her eyesight was bad, that she couldn't see the photograph clearly. Twenty dollars later, her eyesight had improved considerably.

"Oh yeah, that guy," she said. "I can't remember his name and I forgot to get his passport. He paid for a week but didn't even stay one night. He showed up late at night with a couple of people from Ginger's club and they helped him move his stuff."

"Did he say where he was going?"

"No. Nobody tells me anything."

Just then, a pimply teenager in a baseball cap, came into reception and asked the woman behind the counter, in English, whether she had "any stuff."

"For fuck's sake Jamie. I'm talking to a cop. Lieutenant Warren, that's Jamie. Jamie, Lieutenant Warren."

Jamie bowed like he was bowing down to royalty and quickly made an exit.

"Look," Warren said to the receptionist, "if you hear anything about Blake, ring me. I'll make it worth your while." He handed her his card. She shrugged and put it in a drawer that was full of cards.

Warren went back to his cab and asked the driver what he knew about a club called Ginger's.

"It's at the Yumbo. It's one of the gay clubs there. They do a drag show. It's been going for years."

"What time does it open?"

"Not sure. Probably about 8 although most of the bars open at about 11."

"Okay, take me to a hotel."

The cabbie took him to a five-star hotel on the beach, about a fifteen-minute walk to the Yumbo. The Lieutenant needed to check in with his boss. The forensics report should be through by now. He told the driver to park somewhere close and not to take any other fares. He'd be in touch after he spoke to his boss.

"Whatever you say." the driver responded. $500 was sometimes the amount he made in a week. Only a gangster would pay that much. Maybe, just maybe, he had managed to meet his first gangster. He couldn't wait to tell his kids later.

27. Candy, Sweet Candy

Ginger was pissed off. Very pissed off. She was backstage at the club, sitting next to a large suitcase of flour. Her stuff was supposed to be the best in the Playa del Ingles. It wasn't supposed to be flour. She had been ripped off. Nobody ripped off Ginger.

She picked up the phone: "Candy, darling, I'm wondering if you could come to the club. I owe you some money."

"Can't it wait until the show tonight? I'm supposed to be meeting Blake this afternoon."

"Perfect. Why don't you stop here beforehand? I'll be waiting for you."

It wasn't unusual for Ginger to give Candy the money as soon as she checked the coke and made sure it was okay. She didn't like having a lot of money at the club during the daytime. It was a nuisance for Candy who didn't want to take the money to the beach with her when she met Blake. She'd have to go to the club, then back home to drop the money off, and then to the beach. But what Ginger wanted, Ginger got. She called the shots.

When Candy arrived at the club, she was surprised to see Lucca and Manuel there as well. She thought it would just be Ginger. They usually didn't arrive until later to package the stuff up.

"What's up?" Candy asked.

"What do you mean what's up? What the fuck is this?" Ginger opened a suitcase, grabbed a handful of the flour and threw it at her.

"Thanks," Candy said sarcastically as she started to wipe the powder off her clothes. She held some up to her face to take a closer look. "What is it?" she asked.

"*What is it*," Ginger said, imitating what she interpreted as Candy's false sincerity. "You tell me, Missy. What happened to my fucking stuff, bitch?"

Ginger motioned to Manuel who put Candy in a headlock. He squeezed her neck until she nearly blacked out.

"What happened to the stuff, Candy?" Ginger repeated. She had been getting her stuff from the same gang for over ten years and knew they wouldn't rip her off. So, it must have been Candy who substituted the real stuff with flour before dropping it off at the club.

What Ginger didn't know yet was that a major police operation had begun on the island. The cops had already arrested the head of the gang who provided Ginger's stuff. The two flunkies at the bus stop knew that, and decided they needed to get out of Las Palmas before they were next. By substituting the coke that they were given by their boss to give to Candy with flour, they made a substantial amount of money – more than enough for two flights to Calabria where they knew they would be protected. They left the Canaries as free men and considerably richer than when they had arrived. The person who got stung was Ginger and she was blaming Candy.

"What were you planning to do with all that coke?" Ginger asked Candy who was gasping for breath. "Sell it yourself so you could set up house with your new boyfriend?"

She slapped Candy across the face and demanded to know where the dope was. "Did you switch suitcases, you fucking bitch?"

"No, Ginger, you have it all wrong. I did what I always do. Ask Blake."

Ginger nodded to Lucca who slugged Candy in the stomach.

"Don't worry, darling. We'll get to Blake. But if you don't want what we're going to do to you, to happen to him, you better tell us where the stuff is. *Pronto*!"

Candy didn't know what to say. She had no idea what had happened. And now they were threatening to do something to Blake as well. She couldn't let that happen.

"Where's my fucking dope, bitch?" Ginger asked for the third time.

"I DON'T KNOW, Ginger! I really don't know."

Ginger nodded to Rider who undid the headlock and stuck a gun into Candy's mouth.

"Suck on this, *puta*," he said.

"Now Candy, my darling, are you going to tell us what happened or are we going to have to hear it from your boyfriend?" Ginger continued calmly, methodically. She was furious but didn't want to give Candy the satisfaction of seeing her out of control.

"Where's Blake, Candy? Waiting for you at the airport?" she asked.

Rider took the gun out of Candy's throat so she could answer. Candy tried to figure out a way to get hold of the gun but decided it would be impossible to shoot her way out of this without getting shot herself. The only thing she could do was to tell the truth.

"I didn't do anything, Ginger," Candy pleaded. "Neither did Blake. He's not waiting for me at the airport. He's at the beach - in the quiet spot where you and I used to go to drink Cava in the old days. Remember those days, Ginger? When you first rescued me from that other gang? When you were a man?" She knew she shouldn't have mentioned those days, but she was angry. She spat the words out like an accusation, which only made things worse. Ginger had rescued Candy from another gang for a reason. She was in love with her. When Candy had told Blake that she "knew" Ginger had a cock, it wasn't because she had seen her getting dressed backstage, it was because Ginger and Candy had, at one time, been a couple. At least Ginger had been in love with Candy. Candy had pretended to be in love with Ginger so she would help her escape from the previous gang she worked for. After 'saving' Candy, Ginger decided that she would be more profitable as a worker than a lover. It didn't take long for Candy to realise that she had merely traded one type of slavery for another.

She pleaded again, "Blake will vouch for me, Ginger! I didn't do anything."

Ginger grabbed her hair and pulled her head back. "Of course, he'll vouch for you. Why wouldn't he? The two little lovebirds."

"Stop it! You're hurting me! Stop it, you jealous bitch."

"Am I jealous now? I gave up on you a long time ago, lovely. I don't go for whores. *Puta*! she said as she spat in Candy's face.

"Are you fucking crazy? Go find Blake. He'll tell you I didn't double cross you. He's on the beach."

She turned to Manuel: "Kill her."

"Really?" he asked, nervously.

"*Si,* really." She grabbed the pistol out of Manuel's hand and pointed it at Candy's face. "*Really*," she repeated.

Nobody heard the gun go off; a silencer was attached to the barrel. The only noise was the click of the trigger before the back of Candy's head splattered onto the wall behind her. The rest of her body went limp, landing on the floor like a lost dollar bill.

Ginger told Lucca and Manuel to "clean up this mess

¡ahora!" She needed to start getting ready for the first show. It took a while to prepare the stage and even longer to squeeze her large frame into the same red-sequinned dress she had been using for the past ten years. Quite a few of the sequins were gone now, the result of better days gone by, but when the dress caught the lights, it still sparkled.

Lucca and 'Rider' quickly scooped up what was left of Candy and stuffed her into an old steamer trunk that Ginger used as a prop when she mimed a Judy Garland song about being born in a trunk. She would have to perform the song without the trunk at that night's show.

"When you get rid of the trunk," Ginger told them, "Go to the complex and search their apartments - Rider, you search Candy's place; Lucca, you do Blake's. That much cocaine shouldn't be difficult to find. Make sure you go through all their suitcases. When you find it, bring it back here and package it into wraps. I've got enough leftover from last week's drop to supply the clubs for the next few nights, but it won't be long before they start hassling me for more. And hurry up. It will be showtime soon."

Manuel and Lucca had no problem getting rid of Candy's body. It wasn't the first body they had disposed of for Ginger. The few tourists who were on the pavement outside the back of the club took no notice of two stagehands carrying a prop out to Ginger's Range Rover. They drove the car to a marsh of open sewage off the main tourist area that some of the hotels used illegally to dispose of their waste. Dumping Candy's makeshift coffin into the waste, Manual and Lucca put their arms around each other's shoulders like they were at a football game and sang Candy's trademark song as they watched the trunk sink into the swamp of shit: "*Candy, he calls me sugar Candy, because he's sweet on Candy, and Candy is sweet on him...*"

28. A Shadow

While Ginger's thugs watched Candy sink into the illegal mire of waste products, Blake waited for her in the same sunny spot where they had originally met. He lay with his eyes closed on a rented sun lounger, wondering what was taking her so long, and eventually fell asleep. When he woke up and looked at his watch it was already 7:00 pm. The sun was still hot and people were still sunbathing but 'wouldn't Candy be getting ready for the first show by now?' he wondered. He closed his eyes again until a shadow got in the way of his sun and he knew she had finally arrived. He looked up in expectation, but instead of Candy, he saw Lieutenant Warren standing above him. He sat up like a shot.

"Mind if I sit down?" Warren asked.

Blake wasn't about to make room for him on his sun lounger. The sight of the lieutenant standing there, in the same grey raincoat he wore in New York, was more than unsettling, it was surreal. Everything had been going okay before then. For the first time in his life, Blake was in a relationship with a girl he loved. The nightmares he had been having in New York had disappeared. Even if he couldn't make his past disappear, he could at least establish a new routine that would give him a sense of security. He had decided that he would never to go back to New York.

But now Warren had shown up in his grey raincoat and ruined it all. Blake's new world collapsed in an instant. The sunshine, which had felt so liberating at first, now seemed suffocating, like it was burning all the oxygen out of the air.

"What are you doing here?" Blake asked.

"Looking for you." Warren answered.

The lieutenant started to sit down on the edge of the lounger.

"No! Not here for god's sake," Blake warned. "Somebody might see us."

"See us do what? I just want to have a chat."

"NOT HERE!"

"Well, where do you suggest, then?"

Blake had no desire to take Warren to his apartment but couldn't think of an alternative. Besides, if Warren knew where he was on the beach, he probably knew where he was living anyway. The last thing Blake wanted was to be seen with a cop in public. The lieutenant wasn't even trying to disguise himself as a tourist. Who walks around the Playa del Ingles in a grey raincoat? He had 'cop' written all over him.

Blake tried to remember if he had left his works out. He remembered hiding the gun that Ginger had given him under a pillow before he left the apartment that morning but couldn't remember what he had done with his works. The last time he shot up was in the bedroom. As long as he closed the bedroom door when they got to the apartment, it shouldn't be a problem. It also meant that after Warren left, he would be able to check up on Candy. He hoped that she wasn't turning a trick.

Blake stood up and put on his jeans over a pair of red speedos that Candy had loaned him for sunbathing and a light blue polo shirt that he had hung on the back of the lounger. He told Warren to follow him to the boardwalk - but not to walk next to him. When they got there, Warren said he had a car nearby and pointed to his cab. Blake got in, relieved that they were out of the public's view. You never knew who was working for Ginger. Or for Warren, for that matter.

The first thing that Blake noticed in the cab was the driver waving at him in the rear-view mirror.

"Oh my god, it's him!" Blake said as he recognised the driver as the one who picked him up at the airport.

Warren couldn't help laughing. "Yes, I'm afraid it's him, alright."

The driver was overwhelmed to see Blake. "I knew you were somebody important!" he said. He felt like he was on to something big, like in a gangster film. Blake gave him his address.

"The Hellhole," the cabdriver said. He knew the complex by its nickname.

Warren asked, "What the hell is the Hellhole?"

The cabdriver laughed. "Anything but. Luxury holiday apartments, innit?" he said to Blake.

"You could say that," Blake answered.

Warren hoped that the cabdriver wasn't going to get involved in their entire conversation. He needed to tell Blake about Phil and he didn't want to be interrupted.

"Blake," Warren began, "I always seem to be the bearer of bad news."

The first thing that Blake thought of was that something had happened to Candy; that there was a reason she hadn't shown up at the beach.

"Where's Candy?" he asked, panicked.

"Candy? What kind of candy?" Warren asked, wondering if Blake had lost his marbles.

"What's the bad news you have to tell me?

"Phil is dead."

"What do you mean, Phil is dead?"

"Phil Rossi is dead. I thought you were friends."

"How did he die?" Blake asked cautiously, not knowing how much Warren knew or didn't know about their friendship.

"Somebody shot him."

"Who?"

"Me."

"Why?" Blake was incredulous. He knew there were a lot of reasons why a cop would kill Phil but wondered if any of them had to do with him. How much did Warren know?

"After you confessed to the murders, I visited Phil and Susan. "You had implicated them in both murders."

"Confessed?"

"To my colleague - the undercover agent who moved into the room next to yours at the Broadway."

Blake couldn't control his anger.

"How could you do that!"

"I'm sorry Blake, I really am, but we had to get to the truth. My boss was on my case. He was pressuring me to retire. This case was sort of my last harrah. He wanted me to get an alibi from you - or a confession. I planted the agent at the hotel. I figured if there was anybody you would confess to, it would be your mother. She wasn't supposed to have sex with you. It got out of hand. I'm sorry. I really am."

"So, you got your confession. Here I am. Arrest me."

"But that's just it. I never thought you were guilty, so I was surprised when you suddenly confessed."

"But I did do it Warren. I gave José the shot that killed him. I pulled the trigger. And I told Phil about my father's safe and how to get there. I paid for the flights."

"But you also tried to stop the Ridgecrest murder. My boss heard the recording of your conversation with the airline clerk. He told me about it when I checked in with him from my hotel room."

"I never could do a Southern accent."

"And it's not a good idea to pretend to be a driver in L.A. when you're calling from a New York phone number either,

Blake."

"No, I guess not. I've never been a criminal before."

"They busted the Hole in The Wall, Blake. A spotter told them that he saw and heard everything - that Phil gave José the shot. You were too out of it. Think about it. You don't actually remember giving him the shot, do you?"

"Well, no, but I was so stoned, and Phil said..."

"Yeah, Phil said this, and Phil said that, but Phil was wrong. My boss sent someone to speak to Cameron. He had heard Phil's conversation with you and José. It was Phil's idea to go to the Hole in The Wall. Cameron was pissed off about it."

"Good old Cameron."

"It backed up what we learned from Susan when Angela and I went to question her."

"Angela?"

"That was the name of the undercover agent - the same one who pretended to be your mother. You know Blake, I used to have the hots for her. Even when I saw her this time, I was thinking she might be marriage material."

"Is she with you in the Canaries?"

"She's dead, Blake."

"What? I don't get it."

"She tried to save Susan from Phil. He shot both her and Susan. I shot him. Before Susan died, she told me everything - that Phil shot up José. He gloated about it afterwards. And that your father was already dead by the time they got there."

"What do you mean, already dead?"

The driver took a left and drove up the road that led to the Hellhole.

"Your father was into autoerotic asphyxiation, Blake. He had been dead for a few days before Phil got to him. Phil made it look like a murder as a way of controlling you. It was a stupid idea, but it worked, at least temporarily. You didn't go to the police, did you? He also thought the insurance company would be fooled. He assumed that autoerotic asphyxiation wasn't covered by your father's policy and he was right, but he wrong about fooling them. It didn't take long to determine the real cause of death."

Phil tried to process everything that the lieutenant had told him.

"But how did you know I was on the beach?" he asked. "Do you know about Ginger and Candy too?"

"I don't know anything about Ginger and Candy but finding you on the beach wasn't difficult. After I spoke to my boss at the hotel, I decided to take a look around. You weren't difficult to spot, sunbathing on your own like that."

They had reached the gate of the complex. Blake punched in the appropriate code. The gates to Ginger's Hellhole opened up.

"So, Blake, you're innocent. The only witness we have is the spotter and he says you're innocent in regard to José's death. Your father was already dead. Forensics also told my boss that there were prints all over the attic. But they weren't fingerprints. They were sneaker prints - the same sneakers that Phil and Susan had on when they died. Your case won't even go to court, because there's no reason it should. You're innocent."

Blake didn't know what to say. "Innocent," Warren had said. After everything he had been through, he was "innocent." He wouldn't have to spend the rest of his life in prison or on the run. He was free to do whatever he wanted to. Candy would get her picket fence.

Blake was glad that they were going back to his place. The best thing he could do now was to cooperate and tell Warren everything he knew about Ginger. As the cab approached his apartment, he noticed a Range Rover parked outside with the doors still open, as though someone had left it in a hurry. It was Ginger's car.

"Stop here," Blake told the driver. He had to think quick. Who knew what Ginger was up to? He told Warren about his affair with Candy and how Ginger had got him an apartment and a new identity. And how she supplied all the clubs in the Yumbo with cocaine.

"The Spanish authorities know about Ginger," Warren said. "So does the NYPD, now. I don't think she'll be operating much longer."

"That's her car," Blake said. "She must be in my apartment. Wait in the cab and I'll check it out. She'll freak out if she sees me with you."

Blake walked into his apartment. He saw Lucca looking for something, opening closet doors, slashing suitcases with a switchblade, checking underneath the bed. Fortunately, it didn't look like he had checked the bed itself. The pillows were unruffled. The pistol that Ginger gave him must still be there. 'He must be looking for something big' he thought.

"Can I help you?" Blake asked from door leading into the

bedroom.

Lucca stopped looking through the bedroom closet and turned around, surprised by Blake's appearance.

"Where's the stuff?" Lucca asked.

"What stuff?"

"Tell me where the coke is or you're dead," he said as he pulled out a Beretta from a holster covered by his jacket.

"I don't know what you're talking about," Blake said.

"No? You and your drag queen girlfriend don't know what I'm talking about?"

"She's not a fucking drag queen. She's a woman. And who cares anyway?"

"Well, she's a dead woman now," Lucca said. "*Morta!*"

The colour went out of Blake's face. "What do you mean, dead?"

"She's dead, *guapo*. Ginger shot her when she saw those suitcases of flour. Where's the real stuff, *guapo*?"

Blake went crazy when he heard that Candy was dead. "You god-damned mother-fuckers!" he screamed, and then dived onto the bed hoping to retrieve the gun under the pillow. Lucca was momentarily distracted by his action. He fired his gun, but it hit the wall where Blake had been. Blake tried to grab hold of the gun, but the grip was so small that he couldn't get his hand around it. A second shot from Lucca's gun hit him in the back of his head.

"Freeze!" Lieutenant Warren stood at the bedroom door with his own Beretta pointed at the Italian.

"Drop the gun!" he shouted to Lucca who did what he was told.

Wondering what was taking so long, the lieutenant had left the cab and approached the apartment on foot. Blake had left the front door open, and Warren had heard Blake and Lucca arguing. He entered the apartment with his gun drawn. After Lucca dropped his weapon, the lieutenant quickly took an inventory of the room. He saw Blake lying on the bed. He could hear him moaning. He was still alive. Then he heard somebody moving behind him.

"Now, you drop *your* gun, you motherfucker."

The lieutenant turned and saw Ginger, still in the red sequinned dress she wore for her stage show, pointing an AK47 at him.

"What the hell!" Warren shouted as he dropped his gun.

Ginger had sensed something was wrong when she was at the club. She hadn't heard from Manuel and Lucca and when she tried to call them, they weren't picking up their phones. She kept a loaded AK47 in a locked closet backstage – a gift from the head of the syndicate who supplied her with drugs. She grabbed it, put it in a shoulder bag, then took an overcoat from a coat rail and put it on to hide the bag. She jumped on a Vespa that Lucca kept at the club and sped to Candy's apartment. When she saw that the front door of Blake's apartment was open, she went there first.

Standing there with her assault rifle, she knew she was in control of the situation. She was used to being in control. She told the Lieutenant to put his hands behind his head and his nose against the wall. He did what he was told. When she saw Blake bleeding on the bed, she asked Lucca what had happened. As he started to explain, there were three light taps on the opened bedroom door behind Ginger. She turned rapidly around, pointing her rifle at the intruder.

"Um, Mr. Warren, do you still need that cab?" the cabdriver asked Warren who was still facing the wall. His boss had rung him and said he was needed at the airport. He froze when he saw Ginger's assault rifle pointing at him.

"Who the fuck are you?" she demanded to know.

That gave Warren enough time to pull his back-up pistol from underneath his trench coat and point it squarely at Ginger. Lucca, meanwhile, had picked his gun up from the floor and was aiming it at Warren.

"Who's first?" Warren asked, taunting Lucca with his gun pointed at Ginger.

They didn't have to wait long for the answer. A shot rang out and Lucca fell to the floor. Blake had finally managed to get hold of the small pistol under the pillow and shot Lucca dead. Ginger turned her attention from the cabbie to Blake, but she was too late. Warren plugged her with a volley of shots. The rifle went flying as her body jerked in every direction possible, until it finally ended up in a large pool of blood on the floor.

Ginger was dead, Lucca was dead. Blake was alive but barely breathing. Warren was on the phone calling an ambulance. Manuel was in Candy's apartment, smoking a joint. The taxi driver had finally got to see some real gangsters. He was throwing up in the corner of the room.

29. Las Palmas

Blake lay in his hospital bed waiting for his next shot of morphine. He had tried to keep a journal since being admitted a couple of days ago, but it wasn't easy with all of the medication he was on. He had written a little about his childhood but most of the time the notebook sat in the drawer next to his bed. Now that he knew he was going to survive, he had lost interest in it. His nurse, Conchita, had told him he would be out in no time.

"Blake, *mi amigo*, look what I got." It was Conchita, practicing her English as she waved a syringe of morphine at him from his hospital room door. An American nurse was with her.

"Hi Blake. I'm Amanda. The force has shipped me in to make sure you're okay. Looks like Conchita is doing a good job. I'm here to tell you what your situation is and to answer any questions. I'm sure you realise by now that you still have part of a bullet stuck in the back of your skull. They're going to leave it there. It's not creating any problems, although taking it out might. You should be able to lead a completely normal life when you leave here in a week or two."

"That soon?" he said as Conchita injected him.

"Probably," Amanda answered. "We'll need to wean you off the morphine which we've already started doing. After this shot, we'll be giving you oral morphine and then substitute it with codeine. Pretty soon, the only painkiller you'll need will be paracetamol. Until then, the best thing to do is rest. Do you see that chair next to the bed? Sit on it as much as possible. The quicker you get out of bed, the easier it will be for your brain to regain its sense of equilibrium. We'll take you for a short walk later today and starting tomorrow we'll give you physio in the morning and the evening. We need you to get you back into shape for training."

"Training?"

"Oh dear, I've jumped the gun. Lieutenant Warren will here later today and talk to you. Don't worry, you'll get the best care regardless of what happens. Any questions?"

He had tons of questions, but he decided to wait for Warren for the answers. "No questions. I'm going to live. That's all I need to know for now."

She smiled, touched him gently on his arm and said, "You

know, Blake, you're quite a hero. Everyone in the force in New York is talking about you."

"Huh?" The morphine was starting to take effect.

* * * * *

Warren arrived just before noon. Blake was sitting up, awake but groggy.

"Well, my friend, what a ride we've been on," the Lieutenant said. "Thanks for saving my ass. If you hadn't shot Ginger's colleague, I'd be dead by now. And Ginger would still be supplying dope to all the clubs in the Yumbo Centre. You helped to break up one of the biggest dope rings in the Canaries."

Blake tried to concentrate on what he was saying.

"And, even better, my boss kept his promise. I can stay in the force and have an assistant to do all the running around."

So, Blake was a hero. It didn't register. He was thinking of Candy. As if he was reading his mind, the lieutenant said, "Sorry about Candy. I really am. I know you had a soft spot for her. I miss Angela as well. I guess it's all part of being a cop. It's impossible to predict who's going to get lucky. We're the lucky ones, Blake."

Warren paused to let everything sink in. Then he said, "So how about it?"

"How about what?" Blake asked.

"About becoming my assistant."

"Your assistant?" Blake was astonished. He had gone from being a criminal to a hero within such a short period of time. He didn't know which life seemed more like a dream.

"Sure. Why not? You're innocent, Blake. Nobody is going to charge you with anything. For god's sake, you saved my life. If you were a cop, you'd be given a medal."

"Do you mean that you want me to join the force; that if I became your assistant, I'd become a cop?"

"Yeah. I always said you would make a good cop. We want you to go undercover Blake, back to The Broadway Hotel. We want to bust the gang who's been supplying the clubs in Manhattan. Phil was just one dealer among many. We want to get to get to the syndicate at the top of the distribution ladder. You're perfect for the job because you were part of the scene before. Nobody would suspect you. How about it?"

"You know that I used to have a habit?"

"I most certainly do. I saw the blood test when you first arrived. I've already spoken to Amanda about the detox. You won't be the first ex-junkie on the force."

Blake only needed a few seconds to think about it. Of course, he would like to be a cop. He loved watching those old detective shows on television with his mother.

"And I haven't forgotten about your mother," Warren added, as if he was reading Blake's mind. "Don't worry. We'll find her."

"When do I start?"

"As soon as we get you back to New York. There'll be some training, but you'll be working for the force from day one. I'll be back later to go over the specifics. I have to call Seligman and tell him you agreed."

After the lieutenant left, Blake called Conchita over. She'd been fumbling around with his medical records, pretending not to listen to the conversation with Warren.

"Hey Conchita, there's a black notebook in my top drawer. Can you ditch it for me?"

"Dish?" Conchita asked, puzzled.

Blake laughed. "Throw it away in the trash. I never want to see it again."

Conchita got the notebook out of the drawer and held it to her chest, staring at him with admiration. Then she threw it in the bin in his room marked for non-medical waste. She hadn't understood everything that she had overheard, but it was enough to know that Blake wasn't a criminal. He was a hero. She liked a happy ending.

30. Las Vegas

Blake had plenty of time to detox in the Las Palmas hospital as he wasn't due to fly back to New York until mid-January. He didn't mind spending the holidays in the hospital. He had Conchita to keep him company. On Christmas, she even managed to sneak in a bottle of Cava. He couldn't help it - the Cava reminded him of Candy. He wished she was still around. He thought back to the first time they met when she suddenly appeared on the beach gleaming in her sequinned dress, with her opened bottle of Cava.

"To Candy," he said as he held up a glass of Cava from his hospital bed.

Conchita didn't know what he was talking about, but she went along with him and repeated the toast in her heavy Spanish accent - "To Candy," she said.

His American nurse, Amanda, who had stayed to oversee his detox, would have flipped out if she knew he was drinking, but she was busy celebrating her holiday on the beach. Blake had a much better time in the hospital with Conchita - he even met her family who stopped by and brought along another bottle of bubbly and a large lobster dinner. It was the best Christmas he ever had.

It was strange how things worked out. He felt closer to Conchita's family than he had toward his own family. If he did get an inheritance, he would make sure some of it went to her. And he still wanted to give something to José's grandmother - except now he would be able to give it to her legally.

Saying good-bye to Conchita in January was difficult. When she hugged him for the last time, they both had tears in their eyes. He tried to reassure her by saying he would be back, but all she could do was wipe her eyes with her scarf and then use it to wave good-bye as Amanda pushed his wheelchair down the hospital hallway and out the automatic glass doors to a waiting limousine. Blake got first-class treatment all the way to New York, courtesy of his new employer, the NYPD.

Amanda and Blake parted ways once they arrived at JFK. As agents it was better if they weren't seen with each other. Blake took a bus into Manhattan by himself. As the coach approached the city, he felt nervous. He knew he was safe, that Phil and Susan weren't around anymore, but he couldn't help being apprehensive about the future.

He was glad that he had paid his rent at the Broadway for January before he left New York - his old room was waiting for him when he got back. Carlotta was at the front desk, as usual, when he returned. She welcomed him with a suspicious look, especially when he said he wanted to pay for another two months and laid down a large stack of cash.

"Where you been?" she asked. "Workin' on the chain gang?" She had noticed his tan.

"Vegas," he answered.

She nodded. She could believe Vegas. She'd never been there, but wasn't it always sunny in Las Vegas? It was important to remain on good terms with her. Warren had told him she could be a link to the syndicate they hoped to break up.

"You must have hit the jackpot," she said staring at the cash. "You still have your key card?"

"Yes, I still have my key card." Blake took the dented card out of his wallet and showed it to her.

She looked at his large bag and asked if he wanted help getting it to his room.

"If you wait long enough, somebody is bound to come by who can help you."

"No thanks. I can take care of it myself."

He dragged his luggage to his room. When he finally got his key card to work, he opened the door and there it was - his old room just as he had left it. There was still a bottle of whiskey on the table next to the bed. He thought back to his "date" with Angela. Okay, posing as his mother was a dirty trick, but he felt sorry for Warren and his loss. He fell onto the bed, exhausted, and had a restful sleep. No more nightmares.

He woke up the next morning, feeling like a new man with his whole life in front of him. He was "clean" now. The hospital detox hadn't exactly been easy, but it was easier than he thought it was going to be. He never wanted to go back to that part of his life again.

Today was his first official day of training. After he got dressed, he planned on stopping by Gigi's for a coffee so Luigi would know he had returned. It was as important to keep up his friendship with the Italian as it was to stay on good terms with Carlotta. Warren was convinced, although it was mostly a "hunch," that both of them were involved with the mob who were flooding the New York clubs with drugs. If Luigi, or anyone else, asked what he was doing for a job, Blake had been told to say that he was working for a company that didn't exist, in the Empire State Building. The owners of the building were so secretive about the companies that were based there, that it was an easy cover story.

Blake opened the closet in his hotel room to get a suit jacket he had saved from his modelling days. He'd probably be the only recruit to show up in an Armani jacket, but he wanted to make a good impression. He had gained a bit of weight with all that hospital food, but it still fit him. He put his hands in the pockets and stood in front of the mirror to see how he looked. He felt something in one of the pockets. It turned out to be an old wrap of cocaine from his clubbing days. Instead of feeling tempted to try it, he threw it straight into the small trash bin under the sink; it showed how far he had come. To think he had once been excited by that scene! Now, it just brought up bad memories.

'I won't be needing that anymore,' he told himself. He was surprised that Carlotta hadn't gone through the room with a fine-tooth comb while he was away.

He was looking forward to starting his new job - a real job that he could be proud of - none of that modelling nonsense. As he was leaving, he paused as if he had forgotten something, but he couldn't remember what it was. It was like his body remembered something but not his brain. He shut the door and went back into his room. His legs carried him to the bin. It wasn't difficult to find the wrap. He opened it and looked at the contents. He was surprised by the amount - it must have been half a gram or so. He decided that it would be better to throw it out the window then to put it in the trash, just in case Carlotta went through his stuff later. He wasn't even tempted to try it. And even if he did, he knew that it would just be a one-off, that he would never become addicted to drugs again. He supposed that one last line wouldn't hurt - a sort of symbolic good-bye. He could throw the rest of it out the window afterwards.

He used his newly issued NYPD identification card to scrape enough powder from the wrap to make a small line on top of the bedside table. A 'good-bye' line. Then he added more to make a larger line. 'Might as well make the last line worthwhile,' he said to himself.

He took out a twenty-dollar bill from his wallet, rolled it into a tube and snorted the line. He felt the familiar numbness of the drug as it worked its way down the back of his throat and the instant buzz of energy it produced in his brain. There was still a considerable amount left in the wrap and rather than ending up out the window, it somehow ended up in the top drawer of his bedside table.

As he walked down the hotel hallway, he felt GREAT. He was a cop now. A good guy. He looked forward to his first day of training...

[end]

Printed in Great Britain
by Amazon